I0750410

A Walk Among the Shadows: A Firsthand Experience into the Terrors of the Paranormal.

All rights reserved. No part of this publication may be reproduced, stored in a retrieval system, posted on the Internet, or transmitted in any form by any means without the prior written permission of the author. The only exception is brief quotations in printed reviews.

A Walk Among the Shadows: A Firsthand Experience into the Terrors of the Paranormal is a work of nonfiction. Some names and identifying characteristics have been changed to protect privacy. Some elements of certain stories have been slightly exaggerated.

Printed in the United States of America.

www.themichaelandrews.com

Cover design by GermanCreative

Copyright © 2026 Michael Andrews and SoSevere Publishing

All rights reserved.

ISBN: 1737672936

ISBN-13: 978-1-7376729-3-7

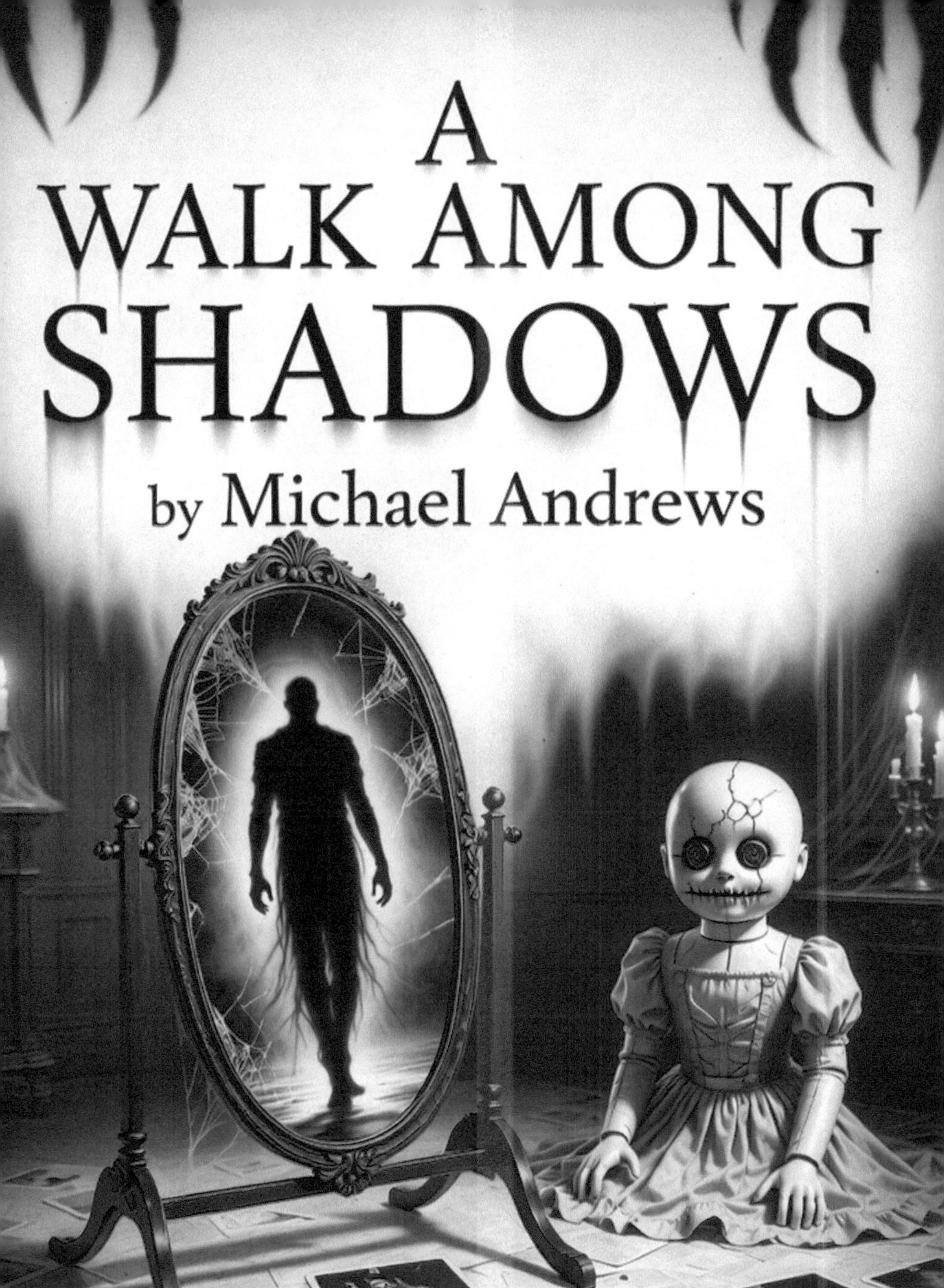
A
WALK AMONG
SHADOWS
by Michael Andrews

Contents

In Memory of

This book is dedicated to my dear friend, Scott Dowd, whose untimely departure from this world has left an irreplaceable void in my life. The weight of your absence has shattered my heart into countless pieces.

Yet, it has also ignited within me a profound urgency to share the insights I have gathered about the hidden realms that exist beyond our ordinary perception.

It's fascinating, almost mysterious, how the universe works. I had intended to publish this book years ago, driven by the desire to share my stories and the dangers of seeking those that shouldn't be sought. But something repeatedly held me back, as if the timing wasn't right.

Now, however, I feel an unmistakable calling: to finally publish and share my personal experiences, which have helped mold me into what I am today.

Before I genuinely found Jesus Christ, I was in awe of the mystical and magical things surrounding our Earth's hidden secrets. And it was that yearning that ultimately showed me how truly terrifying our world really is. But I digress. My good friend Scott started me on this journey many years ago.

So, in loving tribute to your memory, dear friend, I vow to illuminate the shadows with knowledge, awareness, and understanding in honor of you, my cherished friend. I promise to dedicate myself to this journey of enlightenment, knowing that you are with me in spirit, cheering me on.

I will always miss you and will hold forever close the beautiful memories of the incredible times we shared, from our late-night conversations to our spontaneous adventures. Your laughter and wisdom will never fade from my heart. Love you, bro!

Gone too soon but never forgotten in our hearts.

Dedications

Few people come into your life and mean the world to you. Some are seasonal, and some last a lifetime. While we all grow and go our separate ways, some have truly impacted me in such a way that I couldn't even begin to explain. I want to take this time to recognize these friends I consider family. While this book is a counterpart to my Learning to Fly memoir, It serves as a prequel to those events which changed my life.

When I relocated to Southern California, I took nothing with me. Save for some cash and my clothes. I knew no one save for one person. Chris

Hulick. Chris, while it's been a while since we've spoken, I will always keep you close to my heart. You and your family took me in, and you quickly became one of my dearest and best friends. I will never forget the times you were there for me, the times you stayed up late listening to my calls but more importantly, when I'd come over, and we'd hit that Mexican place for some late-night grub. I miss you, brother, and I love you dearly. Thank you for being a stable rock for me in SoCal. Love you, amigo!

To my friend Jenny Smith, towards the end of my tenure in SoCal, you were there for me in more ways than any can imagine. I love you to pieces. Your generosity in my time of need was incredible. I will never forget all those board games we played, those late nights eating good food, spending time with friends, and, most importantly, our weekly game nights. The new friends you showed me kept me afloat when I needed social interaction the most during my dark times, and you are a big reason why I was able to maintain my sanity. Thank you for always being there, and thank you for taking me in. I love you to pieces as well.

To my dear friend and brother in Christ, Adrian Konikow. When the sky got its darkest, and I needed Jesus reinserted back into my life, Jesus led you to me. What you did, I will never forget. Bringing me to church in SoCal, praying with me, the many amazing church events we attended. The singing and praising during our bible studies, etc. Because of you, I reaffirmed my faith and began my journey back to the lord. I will never forget those moments, amigo.

To my brother Gabriel. Thank you for bringing me even closer to the lord and baptized me again in the Holy Spirit. Allowing me to be a part of Salvation in the Streets Ministries and by continuing to pray with me and for me especially through those rough patches I had with my mother. I will always love you brother and words can not express how much you mean to me.

To my mom's cool nurse, Nicky who helped me choose this religious line break for each prayer. Many thanks for the added flair!

And last but not least, to my good friend Mandi. I wasn't going to write this book. It was you who encouraged me big time to do it. That people needed to see this side as well. Thank you for being there. I'm truly honored and glad to have met you all. Many more people have influenced me, and I am genuinely grateful for that. Jesus has been good to me, and now I want to share my story with the rest of the world.

Thank you all again. And to those I've missed, rest assured I have plenty of other books I'm working on with plenty more dedications to follow.

A Letter to the Reader

Thank you for taking the time to read this book. I truly hope that you have enjoyed it. When I first set out to write this I had a compassion to share with you all about the evils of this world. More often than not we take these things as fun and games but there are instances where things can get out of hand. If you have any comments, concerns or stories you would like to share with me or if you are in need of prayer, you can reach me by writing and sending them to contact@themichaelandrew s.com. I will do my absolute best to respond to as many as I can.

Thanks again and take care,

Michael Andrews

www.themichaelandrews.com

www.soseverestudios.com

Prologue

We must all be mindful of the darkness that we traverse. Our journey can be filled with stumbles and falls, and many of us struggle to fully trust in God. Instead of relying on our faith, we crawl through life, failing to realize that all we need to do is trust in Him. By trusting in God, we can turn on our inner light and allow Him to illuminate our path.

Drawing from my personal experiences, my book, Learning to Fly, chronicles my journey from Catholicism to Christianity and how I ultimately regained my faith in Jesus Christ. However, there were moments in my life where my faith wavered, and I made the mistake of seeking answers through means that were unhealthy and led me down a dark path, causing me immense spiritual and emotional turmoil.

As a writer, I feel blessed to have the gift of storytelling. I create intricate worlds that are rich in detail, from the languages spoken to the clothing worn. But I urge others to avoid making the same mistakes I did. Instead, trust in God and rely on your faith rather than searching for answers in the wrong places.

This book has been one of the most challenging pieces I've ever written, not because of the content I'm about to share, but because it reminds me of my past mistakes. It serves as a reminder of my foolish actions and how I naively ventured into things that were beyond my understanding.

Having experienced near-death, I see it as a second chance given to me by God. This opportunity not only allows me to share my story of transformation but also the pivotal moments of my past that led me down a dark path. I am truly grateful for this second chance since not everyone gets this in life. However, I refuse to settle for mediocrity and strive to rise above my previous self.

For some, facing death or the brink of death causes them to spiral into depression. It's like watching Artax's end in the Swamp of Sadness from The NeverEnding Story. If you haven't seen it, I suggest not searching for it on YouTube. The person who wrote and filmed that scene is deserving of some criticism.

But I digress. You see, for me, it was different. Yes, I had those moments of depression, but what made my situation a little different is that, for me, I did die. I died of Covid-19, and what I saw when I died changed me forever. I was always a believer, and my faith in God and Jesus was always stout. In the years since that brush with eternity, God has continued to reveal Himself in extraordinary ways. Two remarkable encounters with angels both profound, undeniable moments of heavenly intervention. These two stories have further solidified my faith, reminding me that His protection and guidance extend far beyond that single turning point. These visitations not only brought awe and peace but also opened my eyes to deeper truths about my own family's spiritual journey, truths I will share in full toward the end of this book

As a human being, I have certainly experienced moments of doubt and uncertainty, questioning why certain events occurred in my life. Life can be unpredictable, and we often find ourselves pondering the "what ifs" and "whys" of our circumstances. It's a perplexing game that we play. Through my own personal experiences, I have come to understand that the world is not always what it appears to be. Walking through life without God is akin to navigating through a minefield. Each step is a gamble, with the potential for destruction lurking around every corner.

It's easy to get caught up in the monotony of our daily routines, utterly oblivious to the hidden dangers that lie beneath the surface. Is this intentional? According to the Bible, some individuals are simply unable to see the truth. I have spent countless hours contemplating this concept, trying to make sense of it all.

As I grew, I began reading various different books on these subjects. Because of my upbringing I never worshiped evil or did anything like that, but I was often curious. From Tarot cards, Forbidden books, psychic mediums, and even the Ouija board it was these very things that opened up doorways that should have never been opened. Passages to realms best left shut and forgotten.

It wasn't until a few years after high school that I became an avid Ghost Hunter. My and friends would often visit extreme locales in search of answers when in truth, the answers which I sought were always right in front of me. I was just too young and naive to understand them. It was these events that shaped and changed me, ultimately leading me down a path that should have never been treated. Why, you say? Because, spiritually, I was broken and vulnerable. I had yet to find my place and calling, and I was nowhere near where I needed to be. It took me dying to fully regain and fill my soul before I truly understood.

So why did this book take so long to write? Why did I not just include it in my Learning to Fly? Well, the answer is simple. I wanted to focus on the person I had become, the person who battled impossible odds with nothing but the faith in Jesus guiding me. The love and faith my family and friends had, but more important, fully letting go and allowing God to navigate my spiritual vessel.

I'll be honest. I never planned this book. But the many people who have read Learning to Fly: Surviving Covid -19 sent me messages and emails and flat out asked me. What are the things you did before that got you to that breaking point? Could you elaborate more and be more precise and in-depth? Others asked about the light that followed and the ways God has affirmed His presence in my life long after I surrendered. It is these recent divine encounters, along with the foundational story of my mother, that complete the picture and show how redemption unfolds over time.

At first, I was hesitant to write this and even considered not doing it altogether. I had written it out, but I needed to decide if I should release it and had even gone back to make some last-minute changes. However, Jesus spoke to me and urged me to share the dangers I experienced so that others could avoid making the same mistakes I did.

Although it was difficult to revisit this painful and long-forgotten part of my life, I knew I had to share it. As a result, you are holding this book in your hands, and I will be recounting events and stories from my life that ultimately led to my demise.

I want to emphasize that everything I will tell you is true and happened to me at some point in my life. To protect the privacy of some individuals, I have changed their names, but the impact of these stories remains the same. I have also changed some of the location areas to prevent others from falling down the same path I did.

My ultimate objective is to uncover the enigmas that lie within the obscure and unfamiliar realm. Through the exploration of the sealed entrances, we may unearth unforeseen realities that differ from our initial assumptions. In the past, I used to be apprehensive of the shadows, but I came to the realization that I am a child of God. A person shining and filled with the light of Jesus Christ and the darkness should now shudder at my radiance.

So, I bring to you now this collection of real-life events which helped shape me from the shadows of my early years, through the valley of death and rebirth, to the recent moments when angels themselves stepped into my path, strengthening what God had already begun. These encounters led me to reflect even more deeply on the origins of it all leading to the powerful, transformative story of my mother whose own walk with the Lord holds the keys to understanding where my light truly comes from.

I do so with a warning. Do not go seeking things evil in nature because you will find them. Thankfully through the grace of God, I was saved, and in the years since, His messengers have reminded me of that truth again and again. So again I reiterate, do not go seeking that which is evil because you will find it and your story may not end up like mine.

There is a Darkness out there. The Shadows beckon all who seek it... but the Light pursues relentlessly, as I've witnessed in ways both past and present and as you'll see when we reach the heart of my family's story.

Nightmare on 969 Oak Street

As a child, I firmly believed that home was a place of love and comfort, but my childhood abode held a dark secret. Time and time again, I witnessed strange and inexplicable sights and sounds that defied all rational explanation. When I turned to my Mother for comfort and guidance, she dismissed my concerns as mere figments of my imagination. But I knew better - something sinister lurked in the shadows of my childhood home, and I was determined to uncover the truth, no matter what it took.

She would say that I was a daydreamer and that my imagination was taking control. Despite her reassurances, I continued to write and draw crazy little stories, setting up army men and transformers and creating movie scenes to act out with my brother. Looking back, I wonder if those stories were trying to tell me something.

Perhaps unconsciously, my mind was trying to issue me a warning. To stay within the boundaries of Phantasia, as they say in the movie The Neverending Story. A place safe from the darkness surrounding every faucet of our lives today. The

Bible warns us that we do not only wrestle with the devil but also against the principles and powers that surround us. These dark secrets lurked beneath the surface of our seemingly idyllic home; I'm sure of that now.

It wasn't until I had a dream so bad that I refused to sleep alone. Technically, I wasn't alone, as my little brother slept in the same room as me. We had twin beds, one on each side of the room. So, I was never truly alone. But he was just a little guy at this time and often slept with my folks.

My sister had her own room and, most of the time, also slept with my Mom as she would often hear noises at night. It was mostly me alone in my room. I remember waking up early one night screaming over a dream I had.

As I closed my eyes, I was transported to a dark and eerie place where the shadows seemed to dance to an unfamiliar tune. A man lurked in the corner, whose face was always shrouded in darkness. His hat was unique, but his crooked smile always sent shivers down my spine. I would try to run, but my feet wouldn't move. Paralyzed with fear, the man's shadowy figure drew closer, and I could feel his icy breath behind me. Suddenly, I would wake up drenched in sweat, gasping for air. Was this a precursor of things to come? Was it an omen? Or was it just a dream? The terror I felt was so absolute that I refused to sleep alone.

So, one day, my Mother took me to a prayer group. It was customary back then. My Grandmother, being a strong church advocate and worker for the local denomination, wanted me to be prayed over. I remember going to these prayer groups and all these little older ladies laying praying hands on me. Some speak Spanish, and others speak in a religious language called tongues, "The Language of God."

I recall one lady falling and almost fainting while she prayed on me. I would later find out that she had told my Mother of a vision she saw. One of me walking with a direct light to God. God had shown her that he would someday use me and that I was truly here for a significant purpose in life.

As a child, I always knew there was something different about me. No, it wasn't anything crazy or weird. It was just a feeling. Like I had a bigger purpose. While I would always play it off and go about my ordinary day, I always felt something missing, like a calling. It was like I was a younger Bruce

Wayne who had looked into a magical mirror to see what I'd become someday. I just couldn't fully nail it.

So, I took those prayers with a grain of salt. As the months passed, weird and crazy things began to happen in that house. Today, my brother, sister, and I laugh at how the address was 969. But back then, things were different.

I recall sleeping one night on the couch and having a dream. A dream of me walking into the small area which housed our washer and dryer. It was a small room roughly the size of a tiny bathroom. This room had two doors. One was a sliding door that led into it, and another a full door that led into the garage.

In this dream, I walked to the sliding door, and as it flew open, something dark pulled me in. It spoke and said that I would never fulfill what I was born for and that it had me forever. I woke up and couldn't move. My chest felt as if something was pressing it down, and I desperately tried to call for help, but no words came out. I panicked badly.

I mean, how could I not panic? I was a little kid witnessing this terrifying event in real time. I layed there prone on the couch, finally getting the words out.

"Mom!"

I screamed. My Mother came running, and all I could do was sit in her lap and cry. I was 6 years old then. As the weeks progressed, my brother and sister would also say they would hear voices in the rooms late at night.

Odd things would also happen. Toilets would flush on their own, and spots would be ice cold despite the heater being on full blast. But what really got the family going was the day my Father witnessed something terrifying.

The first event was a very loud bang on the garage door. We were all in bed with my Mom and Dad that night, and all woke up. My Father jumped, and I remember him grabbing his gun. He walked out and did a perimeter check around the house.

He found nothing. It was late, around 3 a.m., when this happened. When he returned, he said it must have been the wind. But we all knew that the wind doesn't go bang. That next day, I walked over there to see and found scratch marks on the door. It looked as if three fingers had scratched the handle.

I said nothing of it, thinking someone was just trying to break in, but I had heard our dogs barking. The funny thing was that my dog Puggy wouldn't go near that door after the bang. He simply avoided it at all costs.

Then came the event. I call it that because this is when things got weird. It started one night when I was so scared that both me and my brother slept with my Dad. My Mother was in my sister's room with her as my brother and I all started having these dreams.

I remember turning, and when I turned, one of my eyes opened. When it did, I saw what looked like clothes stacked in a small pile roughly an arm's distance away. I wanted to reach out and touch it, but something told me not to. I laid there next to my Dad, prone. I didn't move and kept my one eye half shut and half-open, just staring at what was before me. After a few moments of an intense gaze, whatever it was slowly moved and worked its way out the door. It didn't crawl; it didn't walk or tip-toe. It simply floated out the door.

That next morning, I told no one what I saw. The next few days were fine. No incidents as both me and my bro slept in our beds and my sister with hers. Things were good. But the following day, I overheard my Mom say she had seen a black figure by the door at night. She thought it was me or my brother and told him to return to bed. It didn't. It turned and walked down the hallway to the kitchen. Immediately, my Mother rose up and went to check on us kids. To her amazement, we were all passed out asleep. Just what was that thing? We never knew, but it ended with something that scared the hell out of my Dad.

You see, my Father was a truck driver and would often get home very late. He would eat, shower, and sleep during the week. This often left just me, my brother, and my sister with my Mom. We would eat and lie down watching TV. One night, we were all in the living room, and my Dad was fast asleep. My Mom was in the kitchen when my Dad screamed. We all turned, and he walked out and asked us who had grabbed his legs. Dumbfounded, we all looked at him and didn't say anything. My Mom walked out and told him we were all watching TV, and no one pulled his legs.

My Dad looked terrified as he claimed something pulled his legs while he was sleeping and almost pulled him off the bed. Yes, things like this happen all the time. Again, we were new to this and didn't put much on it. We just thought we were all imagining things.

We resided there for several years, and things more or less stayed the same. While the property was a newer home, an eerie atmosphere was always surrounding it. Although we never saw any truly evil or malevolent activity, we did encounter things that most would consider abnormal.

My Father often claimed to see faces on the tiles that appeared to be looking at him while he was shaving or showering. We all believed he was joking, but we realized he was serious over time. The strange thing was that we all began to witness unusual things. My younger sister would hear whispers in her room at night, and my Mother believed she saw shadows moving in the corners of her eyes.

It was as if the house was alive with some energy we couldn't comprehend.

We tried to ignore it and continue daily, but the peculiar incidents persisted. Doors would open and close on their own, and objects would move inexplicably. As time passed, we grew accustomed to the peculiarity of the house. It became a part of our lives, and we learned to coexist with it. However, deep down, I always pondered what was truly going on in that old house. Was it our imagination, or was something more sinister at work? To this day, I still don't have all the answers. But one thing is sure: that old house will always hold a special place in my heart, and I will never forget the mysterious events we encountered there.

A Circle of Shadow

My obsession with the paranormal didn't start with my own experiences but with a shared one that still haunts me to this very day. Now, if you believe in the existence of a higher power, then it's only natural to believe in the existence of evil as well. But what happens when that evil is so overwhelming that it consumes everything in its path? This is the question that plagued me as I delved deeper into my questions of the darkness that surrounds us. Unfortunately, my quest for answers led me to a story that I'm about to share with you. But be warned - this is not a tale for the faint of heart. It's a story that will leave you trembling with fear and questioning the very fabric of reality.

It all began with an invitation to my friend John's house, which I will never forget. Even though I considered him a dear friend, I never felt comfortable in his home. No, it wasn't his family or him, but he was an amazing friend. He was the type of person who would give his own shirt to someone who needed it. Nor was it his loving family. We loved and still do love John's amazing mother. No, it was just the atmosphere that was off. Something was just different. There was an unshakeable feeling that something was wrong. As I spent more time there and his various other residences as time progressed, I discovered her obsession with the occult.

While she is a firm believer in God now back then before I really knew her John told us that she claimed to be a medium and had all sorts of strange objects, candles, and books related to communicating with the dead. Sometimes, when John invited us over, we would hear her perform seances as the lights flickered in the distance from the home.

I will never forget that fateful night. John invited me and a few other friends for a late-night pool party. When we arrived at John's house, his mom greeted us with a friendly smile and welcomed us inside. She showed us around the house and told us to make ourselves comfortable. She then directed us to the backyard, where John awaited us. As we made our way through the house, we couldn't help but notice the strange smell of incense and the sound of chanting music from the dining room. We looked at each other nervously, wondering what was going on. We could see that the dining room was dimly lit, covered in black cloth, with a large wooden table at the center.

As we entered the room, we were greeted by an eerie sight. The table was adorned with a crystal ball, an Ouija board, and several candles, casting a flickering glow on the walls. The chairs were arranged around the table as if waiting for someone to sit down and take part in some dark ritual. We felt uneasy but decided to keep moving towards the backyard, hoping to shake off the ominous feeling.

John was out in the pool when we arrived in the backyard, enjoying the calm of the evening. We joined him, and for a while, everything seemed normal. We swam, splashed around, and joked with each other. But then, something shifted in the air. The lights in the house began to flicker, and the warm outside air suddenly grew colder. We heard strange noises inside the home, and the air felt heavy with a sense of dread.

We looked back towards the house and saw a shadowy figure move past one of the windows. The figure was indistinct, but we could tell that it was not human. A chill ran down our spines as we realized that we were not alone. The atmosphere was thick with an unsettling energy, and we knew we had stumbled upon something much darker than we had anticipated.

I turned to John and asked:

"What the heck was going on in the house?"

He just laughed and said:

"Oh, that's just my mom. She is having a seance tonight, and the lights always flicker when she's about to start."

This piqued my interest and the interest of one of my female friends who had joined us that evening. We both got out of the pool and went to a window to see what was happening. As we gazed inside the room, we could see John's mom. She was sitting at the head of the table, wearing a long black robe. In front of her was an ornate crystal of some sort. We couldn't fully make it out. Suddenly, the sounds of chantings broke the silence, followed by a blood-curdling "Boo!" that echoed from behind us.

It was so loud and unexpected that we all jumped and screamed in fright. It was John playing with us, asking us what we were doing. I told him I had never seen a seance before and was curious, as was my female friend. He began to explain how they worked and how he sat in on a few before. My friend and I were frozen in fear for a brief moment, unsure of what was happening inside the house. It was as if something sinister had just been unleashed, and we couldn't shake the feeling of dread that had settled over us.

As he continued explaining what was going on in the home, something happened to me. It was like I was in a bubble of some sort. I could hear John telling me what was happening, but my mind was so in tune and fixated on what I was hearing from within the house.

His voice drowned out, and I became fascinated with what was going on. I could barely hear her voice now, but from what I gathered from within the home, his mother was welcoming her guests. I vaguely heard her say.

"Welcome, my friends and family. Tonight, you are in for a treat. I have prepared a special seance for you. We will contact the spirit world and see what messages they have for us."

She gestured for the people inside the house to sit at the table. The guests did so reluctantly, and they all seemed to feel uneasy. She then picked up the crystal and held it before her eyes.

"Let us begin," she said. "I will use this crystal ball to open a portal to the other side. Watch closely, and you will see images of the spirits that want to talk to us."

She closed her eyes and started to mutter some words under her breath. The crystal began to glow faintly and then became brighter and brighter.

We stared at it in awe and fear, wondering what would happen.

Suddenly, we heard a loud scream from behind us; it was our other friends still in the pool.

"Michael, come get your ass into the pool, man, and stop messing around." My friend Mark said.

I was suddenly brought back to full awareness and snapped out of that semi-trance I was under. My female friend and I looked at each other as if we knew something was off.

We then ran into the pool and continued to horse around. It was now getting late. We continued to play in the pool when the beach ball bounced out and headed down a slope, traveling under the crawl space of John's house. John quickly said he'd go retrieve the ball, and we all moved to the hot tub to cap the night. As we sat, we told crazy stories as the night seemed ripe for them having witnessed that crazy séance.

It was late now, and the house lights were all off. Did the seance end? Were they all still partaking in unknown rituals? I had no idea, but those thoughts circled my head, and even though my mind told me to go forth and look, my better judgment at that time said not to. I knew it was late and I should stick with my friends.

We continued to chill and relax when John returned after a few minutes. Only he didn't return with the ball.

He simply replied, "Guys, you will not believe what I just found?"

Games We Shouldnt Play

Our fascination with the unknown is universal. Even though some people try to avoid talking about it, there's a primal instinct at play. It sparks our interest whenever we encounter something that doesn't conform to our standard expectations. Most people deny it, but it happens to all of us. What is this mysterious force that makes us so curious? Could it be our innate sense of Paranormal?

Regardless of what it is, certain things can drive us to engage in activities that we wouldn't usually do, and this very nature can lead us into trouble. I have a story to tell about one such incident.

It happened on a warm summer night, an evening where the air was thick with excitement and fun. I was at my friend John's house with five other people, and we were all splashing around in his pool in the backyard. We were having a great time, throwing a beach ball around, when suddenly it was hit hard enough to roll out of the pool and down a slight slope towards the house.

Back then, my friend's house was still being landscaped in the backyard. The pool was finished, but most of the back was still under development. We laughed as the ball rolled down the slight slope and under the house's crawl space. John jumped out of the pool and said he would retrieve the ball.

We all laughed and decided to move into the attached hot tub. We told scary stories and continued to wait for him when one of our female friends asked what was taking John so long. We all joked some more when John emerged from the background holding an ancient wooden Ouija board.

"Woah, buddy, what do you have there?" I asked him. At that time, I didn't know what he was holding. "Look what I found, guys!" he exclaimed.

As John slowly revealed the object he was holding, our hearts beat in anticipation. It was an ancient wooden ouija board that he had discovered buried deep beneath his house. The board was covered in grime and dust, exuding a strange aura that made us feel uneasy. We couldn't help but wonder what kind of dark and mysterious history lay behind the board and its origins. Our minds were filled with mixed feelings - fear, curiosity, and excitement - as we waited with bated breath to see what would happen next.

While some of us were hesitant at first, I do remember the board giving off this strange, eerie aura around it. But as I alluded to above, curiosity got the better of us, and we decided to play it one night at Mark's house. There were about ten of us now at that time, huddled in the dimly lit family room.

We all had our doubts about touching the board at first. No one wanted to save for John, so I took the initiative and said that I would place my two right fingers on the glass cup. Now, remember that modern Ouija boards come with a marker. Because this was an older, thick wooden one, we had no marker, so we used a small drinking glass instead.

As I placed my fingers on that board, I felt a cold chill run down my spine. The air around us seemed to thicken, and an unnerving silence fell upon us. I tried to keep my composure, but it was hard to do so as an inexplicable feeling of dread washed over me.

We began to ask it questions, and at first, nothing happened. Then John, with a sinister smirk, said some words which I will not repeat here, and the thing began to move. My initial reaction was that John was moving it, but then I asked it a question only I would know, and it moved and answered correctly. The glass moved erratically, spelling out words that made our blood run cold. As the night wore on, the entity became increasingly aggressive, and we knew we had made a grave mistake. We were no longer in control and at the mercy of an evil force.

Now, I knew that John would not know what that answer was, so he clearly didn't move it. And I also knew that I didn't move it either, so it must have moved on its own. These thoughts raced through my mind in a whirlwind of emotion I never wish to remember again.

While John and I were getting a little uneasy, the rest of the group laughed and didn't want to believe that the glass was moving across the board on its own. So we devised a plan. To prove the authenticity of what was going on. We decided that someone who wasn't playing the board would tell us a question they only knew the answer to. John and I would then relay that question to the board. Because we didn't know the answer, there was zero chance of us moving it on our own to guess it.

Well, we shouldn't have done that. As soon as we placed our fingers on the board, an eerie feeling crept up on us. The small drinking glass began to move, but this time it was different. It was as if something far more evil had taken control of it. The small drinking glass started moving in strange configurations, ones which it had never done before. It seemed more possessed now, and we could feel the evil energy emanating and growing from it.

We nervously asked the question, and the board immediately started spelling out words. When it was done, we read it aloud, and our friend, whose question it was, turned pale with terror.

"It's real, everyone. That's the honest truth," he said in a shaky voice.

Suddenly, the room became uncomfortably cold, and we could hear strange whispers and moans coming from the corners of the walls. We all began to freak out and asked our church-going friend to begin to pray. But even his prayers couldn't stop the strange occurrences that followed. The candles flickered and then went out, and the room was plunged into darkness. Suddenly, the board shook violently, and three pictures fell from the wall. We could feel an evil presence in the room and knew we had to end the session quickly. We hurriedly said goodbye to the spirits, but the evil energy lingered, and we knew we had invited something terrible into our lives.

Now, you would figure that this would be the end of this story. But it isn't. Sure, for a while, we never touched that board again. All seemed okay. Things went back to normal, and we always used to mention how funny that night was. Soon, it became a mere afterthought. But yet, our curiosity wasn't satisfied.

It was three months later, and the clock struck 3 am. We found ourselves again at Mark's place, feeling the adrenaline pumping in our veins after a night out at a local party. This was our recap now. A place to unwind and call it an evening. As we talked, John mentioned our experiences with the wooden Ouija board he had found. We all laughed, but our good friends Chuck and Phill didn't believe us.

John spoke up and said:

"I have the board in my car. Let me go get it."

We all laughed, thinking he was joking, but my heart skipped a beat when he returned with the board. Suddenly, someone shouted out:

"Hey Michael, you live near a cemetery. Do you think we should go try it there?"

I replied yes, and the excitement in the room was felt throughout Mark's house. We all discussed the idea of playing it in the cemetery. I mean, what could go wrong, right? Would we really have the courage to do it, though? As we continued to joke around, we finally agreed to try it.

I was inundated with fear but laughed it off, trying to hide my unease, saying:

"Sure, why not?"

So we headed to that local cemetery, with the Ouija board in tow. This time, it was just Phill, John, Mark, Lee, Chuck, and myself. John and Mark were at the board while we stood guard. I remember them sitting on a small marked grave as they began playing. The board wasn't as evil as before, but it still worked. This time, however, the message was consistent. It never answered our questions; it simply kept telling us to leave. But we didn't listen.

Suddenly, Chuck started running out of nowhere, and we all followed suit, not stopping until we reached my car. We caught our breath and saw a man on a motorbike and a girl get off at the cemetery. They didn't look like good people, and we couldn't help but feel like we had escaped something nefarious. Later that night, Chuck confessed that he had seen evil red eyes glowing at him in the cemetery, which was why he ran.

We never fully regrouped to play the Ouija board again. But John was different. The board seemed to have a hold on him. He always wanted to play it, even when we all declined. The board haunted him, a constant reminder of that fateful summer night.

The Cursed Doll

John and I have been tight buds since we first met years ago. We actually met through a mutual friend and hit it off right away. We both loved video games, comics, and horror flicks, so we spent countless hours hanging out at his place with the rest of our crew. We were all obsessed with playing Golden Eye 007; it was our favorite game.

We always made it a point to arrive early and spend quality time together. We loved to unwind by inviting our closest friends over for mini-parties, where we would have snacks and enjoy each other's company. We would also hang out with our buddies, playing video games and watching horror movies. We enjoyed the thrill of being scared and the adrenaline rush that came with it.

One of our favorite things was playing pranks on each other. We never got tired of laughing at each other's reactions. We also loved to tell creepy stories, especially during the nighttime. We would turn off all the lights and light candles to create a spooky atmosphere. The stories we told were always bone-chilling and made our hairs stand on end.

These times were some of the best memories I have. They were filled with fun, laughter, and a sense of camaraderie. These moments will stay with me forever, and I am grateful for our shared experiences.

However, some memories are best left suppressed or locked away. Some that we shouldn't remember. Not because they are wrong but because some stories defy even the weirdest realities and possibilities. How can one truly justify things that are abnormal in nature? You cant! No matter how hard you try, you can't explain these things.

One such thing is the Chucky Doll John had. At the time, it seemed innocent enough. A simple doll we'd joke around with as we smoked, drank, and partied.

While I don't fully remember how John acquired the Chucky doll, all I do know, based on what he told me, is that it was a gag gift he received one Christmas.

The doll looked like the one in the Child's Play movies, with its red hair, blue eyes, and stitched-up face. It even had a voice box that said phrases like "Hi, I'm Chucky, wanna play?" and "I'm your friend to the end!" We found it hilarious and had a great time posing it in different positions all over John's room. We even took pictures with it and shared them with our friends.

Little did we know that those funny memories would be replaced with sheer terror. Things started to get strange after John's mom decided to host a seance in their house. She was interested in the occult and claimed that she could communicate with the spirits of the other side. She invited some friends over, and they set up a table with candles, a crystal ball, and an Ouija board. John and I didn't join them, nor did any of our other friends. Mainly because we thought it was boring and a waste of time. We stayed in his room, playing video games and ignoring the noises coming from downstairs.

We didn't know what happened during the scene, but the lights flickered a few times. It was very similar to when we all partied in the pool. Still, this time, instead of seeing the lights from outside the house, we saw them directly from a first-person point of view on the inside.

I can't explain how the atmosphere was, but it was different. I was looking too much into it, but it felt different, weird, almost surreal. Something was wrong. The hairs on my skin poked up, and we all looked at each other that something wasn't right.

At that time, we just decided to play Golden-eye and forget about it. We could hear the crazy commotion coming from downstairs, so we played some music and gamed away. That night, we all stayed there and passed out with plush pillows and blankets all over the room. It was oddly cold, so John brought in a portable heater, but even that didn't entirely work. John couldn't explain it either because it was colder than average.

Regardless, we smoked a bit and passed out. When we woke up, we noticed that it was no longer cold. We also noticed that the Chucky doll was no longer in the room. This was our first encounter with the Chucky doll acting weirdly. We knew something had gone wrong because no one remembered moving the doll, and no one had entered the room. Instead, we found the doll sitting on the stairs, looking down, hunched over.

Did this damn doll just move? The simple thought of that sent chills down my spine. John snickered, blamed his sister, and kicked the doll down the stairs as a joke. This wasn't the first time we witnessed the relocation of this doll.

Every now and then, the doll would move on its own. It would alter its posture and even speak without us touching the button. There were countless times when we would hang out with no one else around, and we could hear footsteps. We shrugged it off, but we always discovered the doll either sitting in the hallway or lying face down wherever those footsteps originated.

Even though we never witnessed it move with our own eyes, we always felt a sinister vibe from it. Before that seance, the doll was just a harmless toy. But after, we would hear it roaming around the house at night, scraping its plastic feet on the floor. Other times, we would hear it giggling, muttering, or swearing. And sometimes, we would find it saying, "I'm your friend to the end."

Looking back, we should have realized that the doll was possessed by then. We tried to provoke it to talk or move, but it always stayed still and silent in front of us. It wasn't until one of our friends threatened to toss it in the garbage that the doll suddenly burst into laughter.

John turned, and we all followed suit. Our eyes fixated on the doll. It sat there laughing in Chuck's voice. The funny thing was that no one had even touched it. Was it glitching out? Who knows, but the decision was made to get that damn thing out of the house.

John grabbed a bag and placed the doll in it, and we jumped into my car. We drove for almost an hour and eventually worked our way to a Jack in the Box in a small city miles away. We grabbed some food and threw our garbage in the large garbage bin with that accursed doll. We all thought to ourselves that this nightmare was over.

We drove back feeling great. When we arrived back at Johns, we all went into the basement and began playing Golden Eye on the N64. That's when it happened. While we played our usual player-vs-player matches, Proximity Mines, for those who know what I'm talking about, we suddenly all heard a ring at the doorbell.

Now, we didn't think anything of it, as John always had a revolving door, even into the wee hours of the night. We had many friends, and we were always coming and going. The bell rang again, and John and I both walked up. John went into the kitchen to grab some much-needed snacks, and I told him I'd go get the door.

When I got to the door, I looked through the peephole and didn't see anyone. My initial reaction was that it must have been either someone playing a prank, as the neighborhood was filled with kids, or whomever it was had left. I turned and headed towards the steps that led back down to the basement area. John met me halfway when the doorbell rang again. I told him that I had looked, and no one was there.

Confused, we both walked back to the door, and both checked, and nothing. Suddenly, again, the doorbell rang, and we both jumped. We looked at each other again, very confused. John finally said we had to open that door, so he opened it, and sitting on the doorstep was the Chucky doll.

Now, this wasn't very clear. How did the doll get here? We drove for an hour to a small town and told nothing about what we were doing. The Jack in the Box parking lot was empty save for the employee cars. We ate in my car, and no one else was there. When we tossed our garbage and the doll, the parking lot was empty of people. So what the heck was going on here? Thoughts of Carol-Anne saying, "They're here," began rounding in my head.

Regardless, we had no answers. The doll stood there looking at us. And that's when the voice in the doll kicked in laughing again. It was as if it knew what we were thinking and was mocking us. John picked up the doll, and we both worked our way to the basement. Everyone was shocked at what we showed them.

For a while, we pondered what was going on. Finally, we all decided the best thing to do was lock the doll up and surround it with holy objects. So that's exactly what we did. Since then, the doll has never moved and has been in my good friend's closet. When I ask him if the doll has done anything, he says it hasn't. To this very day, I have always wondered about that doll.

Let Me In ...

These are the types of stories that send shivers down my spine. They remind me of a dark time in my past that I have fought so very hard to forget. I hate writing them because they are true and bring back memories that I have tried to bury deep in my mind. There were many things I did that I regret and some that I can hardly believe I was capable of. It's a scary thought to think that the person I was back then still exists somewhere inside me.

These memories haunt me because they remind me of how easily we can lose ourselves in the midst of chaos and confusion. They warn of how quickly we can become someone we don't recognize and how difficult it can be to come back from that dark place. The fear of losing control is a powerful force, and it still grips me to this day.

But as much as these memories scare me, I know they are a part of who I am. They have shaped me into the person I am today, and I wouldn't be where I am now without them. They have given me character and taught me valuable lessons that I carry with me every day. In a way, they have become a source of strength, a reminder that I am capable of overcoming even the darkest of times.

So yes, these stories are scary, but they are also a testament to the resilience of the human spirit. They remind us that we are all capable of change and that even in the darkest moments, there is always hope for a better tomorrow.

For a long time, I was a skeptic about the existence of ghosts. I had heard stories and rumors about these otherworldly beings, but I always dismissed them as nonsense. That all changed when I experienced something truly terrifying that shook my beliefs to their core. As you read before this segment, it started when I was a child growing up, witnessing things and seeing things that just didn't make sense.

As I grew older, some of these things intensified. But what really changed it all for me was when the Paranormal became Metaphysical. That began when my friend and I decided to embark on a ghost-hunting adventure in a small southern Californian town. The place was surrounded by forgotten tales and whispers of supernatural occurrences.

We were both thrill-seekers and were excited to explore this quaint and almost desolate place. As we arrived in the town, we felt strange energy in the air. It was as if something was watching us, following our every move. We shrugged it off as our imagination and continued on our journey. The first night, we camped in an abandoned house on the outskirts of town.

As we were getting ready to sleep, we heard strange noises coming from the walls. It sounded like whispers, but we couldn't understand what they were saying. We tried to ignore it and went to sleep, but I couldn't shake off the feeling that something was in the room with us. The next day, we explored the town and talked to the locals about their experiences with ghosts. Many of them had spine-chilling stories to tell us, and we realized that this place was truly haunted.

The sun was setting now, casting long, eerie shadows that danced with the wind. We decided to turn it in for the evening, but we wanted something quick to eat before then. The town was quiet now, save for the occasional rustling of leaves and the distant hum of a fast-food joint, our chosen spot for a quick meal. The place was nearly empty, a testament to the town's size and the hour.

As we returned to our car, the glow of the setting sun illuminating the deserted streets, we noticed a group of three children slowly making their way towards us. Their faces were shrouded in shadow, and they moved with a strange, almost inhuman gait. At first glance, they seemed like ordinary kids, perhaps homeless and hungry. But as they drew closer, the atmosphere shifted. An icy chill ran down our spines, and the hairs on the back of our necks stood on end. Their movements seemed well calculated, and we couldn't shake off the feeling that something was terribly wrong. An uneasy chill ran down our spines, a primal warning that something was amiss.

I began to start the car when one of the children, who happened to be the tallest among them, approached our car and tapped on the window. He spoke softly, almost in a whisper, asking if they could get a ride. My friend, who was moved by their apparent plight, was just about to unlock the doors when I stopped her. I had noticed something odd about their eyes; they seemed different.

My friend turned to me and said:

"What's wrong, Mike?" "They are just kids. Maybe they just need a ride home and are scared of the evening coming."

I looked through my friend directly at the kids. Upon closer inspection, I realized with a jolt of fear that the eyes of the tallest kid were completely black, devoid of any white or color. It was as if we were staring into an abyss, a void that seemed to consume all light and hope. The realization hit me like a cold wave, sending shivers down our spines.

I quickly grabbed my friend's hand and prevented her from opening the door. She stared at me in a confused daze and again asked:

"Mike, what's wrong, man?"

I told her to look at their eyes very calmly but remain calm. I had heard stories of these types of encounters, and as long as we remained in the car and never invited them in, we would be okay. She turned, and I immediately felt her hand turn stiff and cold. We both looked at each other, and I said:

"God's with us; we shouldn't fear them." "Just follow my lead. Do you trust me?"

She nodded and remained calm, but I knew she was beyond scared. I mean, how could she not be. We sat for a minute as the kids kept saying things like.

"C'mon, guys, we're cold. Let us in." "We just want a ride back to our homes." "Please help us."

We ignored them, and I told my friend to begin praying with me. So we began. As our prayers intensified, I could hear the older kid begin to get frustrated. He was now banging on our door enough to shake it a bit.

"Let us in now!"

We continued to ignore him and the others and continued with our prayers. As we prayed, we closed our eyes so we could not see what was going on outside. After a short while of intense prayer, we suddenly both felt a sense of calamity. We no longer heard the kids. We both opened our eyes, and the kids were gone. Not wanting to stick around, I quickly started the car, the engine's roar shattering the eerie silence, and we drove away.

As we drove, I gestured we were not staying in this town. We drove a few hours to the next major city and booked a nice room. As we drove through, we could still feel their black-eyed gaze piercing through the rearview mirror, a chilling reminder of the encounter. The ghost hunt had taken an unexpected turn, leading us to a haunting encounter with the black-eyed children of the small southern town.

As we cuddled together in that room, fear raced in our hearts as they pounded when we recalled what we had just witnessed. We made a pact to keep this story buried deep within us, never to be uttered to another soul. But the memory of that night still haunts me, and I can no longer keep it to myself. Evil lurks in the shadows, waiting to pounce on the unsuspecting. And when you go searching for it, you may just find yourself stumbling upon something far more terrifying than you ever imagined. This is my first time sharing this story, and I can feel the chill creeping down my spine as I do so.

The Gates of Hell

I still have nightmares about that night. The night my friends and I decided to explore the Gates of Hell was supposed to be a fun adventure, a dare to test our courage. But it turned out to be the most terrifying experience of our lives.

The Gates of Hell was a dead-end road in the countryside, blocked by a small gate and two massive pillars. It led to an old asylum in the mountains. While we don't know for sure what went on there, the idea was that something terrible had happened, as the place had been closed down and the road gated up.

We grew up with the Gates of Hell, a place that terrified us kids. But despite all the rumors and crazy things said, people still went there late at night. Perhaps it was the drive to get there. At the time, it was more countryside than anything- a long, twisted, dark road with no lights save for your car's headlights, the only illumination coming from the soft lunar glow if the moon decided to show its face.

We often visited that place, and it was always a thrill until that one series of nights that I'll never forget. While we never did truly believe any of that, of course. We were just curious and bored teenagers looking for a thrill. So we drove to the Gates of Hell one evening, just before sunset. We parked our cars near the gate and got out. There were six of us: me, Mark, Scott, Lisa, Amy, and Phil. We had flashlights, our older beepers, and lighters for light. We thought we were prepared for anything.

We climbed over the gate and started walking down the road. It was a long, winding path surrounded by tall grass and countryside. The sun was setting behind the mountains, casting an eerie glow over the landscape. We could see the asylum in the distance, a large, imposing building with broken windows and a rusty roof.

We joked and laughed as we walked, trying to scare each other with stories and sounds. We didn't notice how dark it was getting or how quiet it was. We didn't notice the strange smell or the cold breeze that made us shiver. We noticed something when we got close to the asylum.

That's when we saw the lights. They flickered and flashed inside the building like a disco ball. They were different colors: red, blue, green, yellow, and purple. They moved and changed like a kaleidoscope. They were mesmerizing and hypnotic. We stopped and stared, wondering what they were. We took out our cameras and tried to capture them, but they didn't appear on the screen. We felt a strange attraction to them, like moths to a flame. We wanted to go inside and see them for ourselves. But then we heard the noises.

They were loud and horrible, like nothing we had ever heard before. There were growls, howls, and screams. We began to wonder if they were animal, human, or something else. They came from inside the asylum and the tall grass around us.

We panicked and ran, dropping our flashlights and cameras. We no longer cared about the lights; we just wanted to escape. We sprinted back to the gate, hoping that nothing would catch us. We heard something rustling in the grass, something big and fast. We heard it breathing and snarling, getting closer and closer.

We reached the gate and climbed over it, barely escaping the thing that was chasing us. We got into our cars and slammed the doors, locking them. We started the engines and drove away as fast as we could. We didn't look back or want to see what was behind us.

We jumped in our cars and began laughing at what idiots we were. We may have envisioned something more than what it really was. We assumed it was far worse because of the isolation out in the mountainside. The layout of that stretch of road was quite unique. It had the Gates of Hell, but not too far down the road, it forked off to an old, abandoned slaughterhouse. We stopped and decided to walk around to regain our barring.

I know what you're saying. Wow, these kids are stupid. That's your mentality growing up, like you're invincible and untouchable. As we walked around, there was a small, broken, and falling apart homestead. It appeared to be the home of the person who ran the old mill and slaughterhouse.

We walked inside, and a few walked up to the slaughterhouse. We eventually all ended up walking around the old mill. It was broken and open, so it wasn't like we were enclosed. The eerie cascade of moon glow and shadows would have scared the average person, yet we persisted.

The girls with us loved it. They were scared, but they knew that we guys would be there. Typical "I know what you did last summer" stuff. As we walked around, we noticed strange footprints. It was probably coyotes, as they were always spotted and seen during the day by anyone who would drive down that road.

We eventually had our fix and decided to continue down the road. Not far from that mill was a mile-long road called Gravity Hill Road. Crazy, right? The Gates of hell, an old beat-up slaughterhouse mill, and a road called Gravity Hill all within four miles of each other.

Now, the urban legends of our town claimed that this was a road where cars would randomly stop. When stopped, they would begin to roll forward. Many claimed it was an optical illusion. I called bullshit simply because the road was straight.

Cars began to move and eventually reached a top speed of 15mph. How could that be possible on a straight road? To make things even more crazy, the cars continued at that speed, never going above or below, and at a certain point, they stopped.

The legend here was that many years ago, a bus carrying children crashed. All the children perished, and now the cars are pushed by the children to pull them to safety. An urban legend? Perhaps, but regardless, we continued down that stretch of road.

As we approached that segment, our cars suddenly stopped, as if they had run out of gas. We tried to restart them, but they wouldn't budge. We freaked out and exited our cars, wondering what was happening. That's when we noticed the hand prints.

They were small and weird, like a child's, but they were not human. They had long fingers and sharp claws. They were all over our trunks as if something had climbed on them. They were fresh and wet as if they were still there. We screamed and ran back into our cars, not even questioning what we saw. I recall the girls screaming for me to start the car. Eventually, the car started, and we raced back to my buddy Mark's house.

We stayed at his house for the night but couldn't sleep. We kept hearing the noises, seeing the lights, and feeling the hand prints. Even though we were in the comfort of a home, we still felt as if parts of us were still there. We kept wondering what we saw. What were those lights in the asylum? Had we been warned off? Did it follow us to the slaughterhouse?

While the slaughterhouse was scary, it didn't seem like it posed any danger, but it still felt weird. And what happened on Gravity Road? Did we just freak out over some random car issue? My car wasn't exactly brand new. Or did we really witness something? Something far more sinister than anything.

We kept wondering if we were safe or if they would find us. The next day, we returned to the Gates of Hell, hoping to find some closure, but we went in the daylight this time. We found tiny dolls at the gate, hanging from the pillars. They looked like us but twisted and distorted. They had buttons for eyes and stitches for mouths. They had needles and pins stuck in them and blood dripping from them. They looked like someone had placed a spell or something on them.

We were shocked and scared, and we wanted to leave. But we also wanted to know what was going on. We wanted to solve the mystery and end the horror. We wanted to venture down the road again and face whatever was there. We climbed over the gate, ignoring the dolls. We walked down the road, ignoring the noises, but we never reached the asylum. Instead, we decided it was best to just leave and never come back.

The next day, in the newspaper, we read about a small fire in those foothills. It burned down the asylum and everything around it. It was caused by a lightning strike, or so they said. It was a freak accident, or so they said. It was a tragedy, or so they said. But we knew the truth. We knew that the fire was not an accident but a warning- a warning to stay away from the Gates of Hell and never come back- a warning that we ignored and paid the price for.

To this day, we still wonder what truly happened. We still wonder what those lights, noises, and handprints were. We still wonder what those dolls were and what their purpose was. The place is blocked off. Forbidden. The entire 4-mile stretch of road is unreachable now. Surrounding it is an urban community of homes. Many not knowing that just down the countryside there exists an urban legend which terrified us as kids.

It's been years since I last walked the streets of my childhood neighborhood, yet the memories are still vivid. While the city and its citizens may have forgotten, as most things are, those of us who grew up there know firsthand what lies beyond the community of homes.

The stories were always different, but they all shared a common thread - the evil that lurked beyond the gates. Some say that the spirits of those who died in the house still haunt the property, while others claim that the gates themselves were a portal to a demonic realm.

Regardless of the tale, one thing was certain - no one dared to venture beyond the gates. We were just too naive to understand the idiocy of our doings. Even now, as an adult, I can't help but wonder what really lies beyond those gates. The fear and uncertainty I felt as a child still lingers, a testament to the power of the urban legends passed down between generations that we told each other.

Whatever it is or was, I will never know. All I know now is that the place is sealed. Sometimes it's better that way. A place locked behind the recesses of our memory in urban legends about our local area, a place we called The Gates of Hell.

The Black Mirror

They say that every family has an object—a heirloom of mystical energies—something that has been passed down from generation to generation. Often, these objects are so old that one simply can not remember when or whom in the family the item first presented itself.

Most often, these are pictures or small objects—objects forgotten and lost in time but remembered by those who keep passing them on from one generation to the next.

My family has such items, but ours are more holy than anything. One of them is an old rosary that my grandma's grandmother had and an old oil painting of Jesus from the Vatican that was passed down and is now in my possession.

These items not only bring significant person value but also spiritual value. But what happens if some of these items aren't good? What happens if some of these items border the realm of horror and terror? What if these items are passed down but done so not for their historical intrinsic value but for a family to simply protect the outside world from obtaining them? Thus, These families become the custodians of the things that truly go "Bump" in the night.

I will never forget the Black Mirror. I remember reading stories about how black mirrors existed throughout history. Some of the world's most famous and ancient theologians and seers had them. In fact, it was fabled that the great Nostradamus had a black mirror where he would gaze and see images of the future?

Are these objects of divinity? Are they objects of lies and evil? Perhaps they are simply portals or gateways to the unknown universes and parallel dimensions that exist and surround our world and that we can not see. Science has proven that there are more than just the dimensions that we live in and are aware of.

These mirrors allow us, however, so briefly, to gaze into the unknown. Unbeknownst to us that while, doing so could open us up to things we should never play with. I admit I was naive then. While I believed in God, as I alluded to with my other stories, I still struggled with these things. They piqued my curiosity in ways where the adrenaline would rush through my veins. I was possessed. No, not like that crazy gal whose head spun like a record player as she vomited green ooze everywhere. We all know that movie. I was really into the thought that these things existed, and I had to learn more about them.

I will never forget that night when I first gazed upon a black mirror that had been a part of a friend's family for years. The thing is, my friend whom it belonged to didn't know how long it had been in the family. All they knew was that it came from their grandparents' estate. I remember it clearly now.

The night was young, and the air was filled with the kind of electricity that only comes with new friendships and unexpected adventures. I had been invited to a small gathering at the home of some friends I had recently met. The way I met them was kind of cool, actually. I won't get into details, but they became lifelong friends. But I digress. Soon after meeting them, my boys and I would often meet up with them, and we would just party at each other's houses.

Their house was an older home in a nearby city, with the kind of charm that whispered stories of the past through its creaking floors and drafty windows. While the home itself was safe and not ominous at all, the black mirror changed everything.

Walking into that home was basic. It had a nice older common structure. When you walked in, immediately to the left was the family room and a long hallway leading into the bedrooms. To the right was the living room and a large kitchen, which led into the backyard entrance. As I said, it was a common and very comfortable place. I didn't get any uneasy feelings at all. In fact, we had partied there before without incident numerous times.

As I mingled and laughed, my eyes were drawn to an oddity in the family room—a large mirror covered with a heavy, dark cloth. It seemed out of place, like a secret begging to be told. Curiosity got the better of me, and I asked about it. "Oh, that old thing?" one of the girls replied with a shiver. "It's haunted. We keep it covered for a reason."

As soon as she said that I was locked in, I wondered what made it haunted. Why cover it? What kind of mirror was it? I was beyond curious now. I asked more questions, but my friend seemed to disregard them. No, not in a bad way, but more of like, I really don't wish to talk about it.

As the night wore on, I couldn't stop thinking about it. Why was it covered? I asked myself again. The sheer curiosity got the best of me again, and I began to ask more questions.

" So how do you know it's haunted?"

"has anything happened before with it?"

Again, my questions were shrugged off.

"We just don't talk about it." My friend answered briskly.

She then started mingling with friends, and at that point, I figured I'd either find out later or just take a look once everyone passed out.

As the night progressed, we had fun. We enjoyed mixed drinks, stories, and laughs—a typical small gathering of young, almost 20-year-olds. But as the night went on, I still couldn't get it out of my head.

Just what did the mirror look like? Was it basic? Was it ancient? Regardless, I kept partying until the party dwindled, and the sounds of celebration were replaced by the deep, rhythmic breathing of those who had surrendered to sleep. But sleep eluded me, and I wasn't alone. One of the girls, a cousin of the house's original owners, sat wide-eyed in the dim light.

We talked for a bit, and I motioned for her to come sit next to me on a small couch in the room.

The others had all passed out on the floor in an assortment of pillows and blankets, punch-drunk from the fabulous drinks we had enjoyed just hours earlier.

"So what's with that mirror?" I humbly asked.

"Oh, that thing, it's been in our family for a long time. My mother didn't want it, so it came here."

I thought to myself, okay that's strange, but not out of the realm of possibility. I mean, sometimes people don't want stuff. I get it. But still, I asked more questions.

She began to tell me that she didn't know where it came from but that what she was told was to stay away from it. We both began to laugh. It was then we heard a slight whimpering voice coming from the other room.

"Do you hear that?" she whispered, her gaze fixed on the shrouded mirror.

I did hear it—a faint, almost imperceptible murmur slash whimper, like a small child crying, but it sounded distant. I looked at her, and she looked at me. As we gazed into each other's eyes, we fell in love! Okay, we didn't fall in love, but we did share a brief moment of wtf!

Again, we heard a child crying, and we stood up.

"Okay, I definitely heard that," I said

She shook her head in confirmation. I grabbed her hand and began inching closer to the covered mirror. Driven by a mix of fear and fascination, we approached the mirror. My hands trembled as I reached for the cloth, and with a swift motion, I unveiled the glass.

Black. It was utterly black as if it absorbed all light and hope. My reflection was nowhere to be seen, just an abyss that seemed to stare back into my soul. Panic gripped me, but the girl remained calm.

"It's been in our family for generations," she said, her voice steady but low.

"No one knows where it came from, but every night at 3 a.m., you can hear whispers and the sound of children crying."

I glanced at the clock—2:58 a.m. The murmurs grew louder, and a chill ran down my spine.

"Sometimes," she continued, "I've been told that you can see the silhouettes of children running towards the mirror as if it's a portal to another world."

While my heart said bullshit, my mind heard what it did. And the fact that it didn't cast any reflections also had me on edge. SuddenlySuddenly, the clock struck 3 a.m., and the room was filled with the unmistakable sound of weeping. I looked into the mirror, and though it remained black as pitch, the cries of unseen children echoed around us. We quickly covered the mirror, and the room fell silent.

We hurried back to the couch, and she asked if she could sleep next to me as we both felt uncomfortable. We literally held each other all night until we finally fell asleep after hearing nothing for a while.

We never spoke of that night again, but the memory lingered, haunting my dreams. The mirror remained covered, a barrier between us and the unknown, a keeper of secrets never meant to be uncovered.

A Price for Fortune

Many are familiar with items of divination. Items that supposedly can tell the future or guide you. As a believer in God, I knew better. However, because my faith was weaker then, I always questioned everything. I'd often call mediums or have my cards read, not realizing the ramifications of my actions. They say that for every action, there is an equal opposite reaction. Looking back, I realize how stupid I was in believing these things. I would have never touched those things if I had known what I know now. I put my full faith in God now.

But back then, things sure were different. In one of the most terrifying experiences I am about to share, I now know how real these things can be. Despite everything I had seen, I never knew the power certain items held. I know now that the truest power comes from the faith in the cross of Jesus, but back then, I wasn't so inclined to believe that.

I always poked fun at the tarot card readings I often got at local fairs. It wasn't until a close friend of mine told me about some cards he needed help destroying that I really became interested. I'll always remember how that story unfolded.

It was late at night, and we were all playing an old board game. As we sat, we drank and joked around when the topic of the paranormal came up. My friend Blue began weaving a tale about these cursed tarot cards.

"Cursed," I said excitedly.

"Yes, amigo, cursed beyond anything imaginable."

Blue continued telling his tale as we all dropped what we were doing and focused all our attention on him. As he spoke, he wove a crazy tale of how his dear friend's mother had inherited the cards from her late grandmother. The cards were ancient, their edges frayed, and their illustrations faded. Blue's eyes held a mix of awe and trepidation as he recounted their history—the tale passed down through generations of women in his family.

"Now, everyone," he said, his voice hushed, "these cards carried with them a curse. A pact made long ago by my friend's ancestors."

We couldn't believe what was being said, but Blue carried on.

"That curse was that whoever possessed the cards gained wealth beyond imagination, but it came at a terrible cost—the lives of the men in our bloodline."

I raised an eyebrow. "Men die for riches? Sounds like a grim fairy tale."

Blue shook his head. "It's no fairy tale."

"A very close friend of mine told me that she needed help. Her great-aunt Amy held these cards during the stock market crash of '29. She became a millionaire overnight, but her husband perished in a horrible accident the very next day."

I stopped him from talking and began to ask many questions. How could playing Tarot cards do this? You see, I have friends who use them frequently. I'll admit that during that time in my life, I had my cards read once or twice. I am not a fan of cards telling one's fate. We choose our own destinies. Yet the thought of cards having such a profound effect intrigued me.

He continued to tell the story, and we all just listened. When he finished, I thought that what he had told us was a crazy bedtime story, just one of those old experience-type stories we all share and love to tell. Little did I know that this story would directly impact me and become all too real.

A few months passed, and we scarcely heard from Blue. He was much older than us, so we figured he was enjoying his retirement or relaxing. When we finally heard from him, it was a conversation that would change my way of thinking about tarot cards forever.

As I said, I never took these cards that seriously. I had friends who used them, and I would ask them to give me a reading or two, but I never placed anything on them. I believe in God and don't believe in how objects like these can tell you what's going to happen.

But my faith wasn't like it is now. Back then, I wasn't full of the Holy Spirit yet. I was simply a man seeking the unknown. And while I enjoyed that kind of stuff, it's a totally different feeling when you go looking for it. As the saying goes, be careful what you look for; you may find it.

But I digress, back to Blue. When Blue came back, we all asked him how he was doing, and that's when I pulled me to the side and asked if we could speak a bit.

Now, Blue knew what I did then: ghost hunting, paranormal research, and stuff. So he knew I would take him seriously if need be. We walked, and he told me he was busy handling personal business.

I sat and continued to listen. As Blue went on, he told me what exactly he was doing. It turns out that his friend's grandma was getting old, and when the time came to pass the cards, she had gifted them to his friend's mother. Now, the time had come to pass the cards to Blue's friend.

I responded. "The ones that Amy passed on, the cards from 1929?"

Blue nodded and said, "Yes, those very cards." "They have since been handed down, and now my friend's mother was in possession of them and had gifted them to her."

I continued to listen. He told me his friend didn't want to believe that the cards held such power, and things started happening. She won small amounts in lottery tickets, eventually winning 50k. After that, she became suspicious. She got a promotion at work and was making alot of money now. Things looked bright for her but something was odd about this.

That's when the bad started to happen. First, her husband got sick and died of his illness. She didn't think that was too far-fetched, but when her son got hurt and began getting sick, she started second-guessing the cards.

Blue continued and said that when her son got sick, she finally broke down to him and didn't know what to do. That's when Blue made the decision for her: to get rid of the cards by dousing them in holy water and then burning them. I agreed and promised to be there if needed. I brought some plastic rosaries that my grandmother had given me, blessed ones, and some holy oil and water.

We met at her home, and when we walked in, Blue introduced us. She again gave me a brief summary of the cards, and I asked to see them. She took them out of an old ornate box. The cards were wrapped in cloth, and as she removed them, I saw them for the first time.

They looked different from any other basic tarot cards I had ever seen. No, there was something different with these cards. The air got stale quick. Blue and I both felt the change. His friend looked at us and said we have to do something.

I picked them up and held them for a minute. Their design was insane. As I traced my fingers over the worn symbols—the Fool, the Tower, Death, I felt a sense of unrest. I placed them into the small fireplace as we decided to destroy the cursed deck.

"Ready?" I asked as I began placing the rosaries and sprinkling the holy water and oil over all the cards.

Blues friend hesitated, then nodded. "Let's end this."

"It's for the best," I assured her. "We're breaking the cycle."

"This ends now."

To our amazement, the cards would not burn. We kept lighting the fire and throwing more kindling into the flame, but nothing. The cards sat there as if protected by some unseen force.

Regardless, we persisted, as the cards needed to be destroyed. Eventually, the cards began to burn, at which point the flame turned blue, and we heard a loud shriek. It scared us, as we had never seen or heard anything like this.

As time passed, the cards continued to burn. Finally, the last card met its demise. The flames roared, and the tarot deck let out a final wail. The fire consumed them, leaving behind only ashes and a lingering sense of release.

Blues friend collapsed, tears streaming down her face. "It's done," she whispered. "No more curses."

But the cards weren't finished. As the last ember faded, they shrieked a final time. The flames danced higher, defying the laws of physics. And then, with a burst of crazy blue light, it was all over.

We stood there, breathless witnesses to the end of a cursed legacy. The air smelled of burnt paper and redemption. Blue and I looked at each other, not believing what we had just witnessed. His friend hugged us both and said.

"Thank you for helping me break free."

As dawn approached, we buried the ashes beneath an ancient oak tree. The curse was broken, but its memory lingered—a cautionary tale of greed and sacrifice.

Later, we heard how her son miraculously recovered. We were relieved. I will never forget this experience with cards and vowed never to touch them again. Sometimes, on moonless nights, I swear I hear the echo of those shrieking cards, a reminder that some secrets burn brighter than any flame and are better left alone.

An Unholy Cemetary

I remember that summer quite well. It was during a time of my life were I wanted to simply explore strange things. Some of my friends and I got obsessed with exploring abandoned places. Where I lived wasn't too far from San Diego, so we'd already hit up the usual spots. Old warehouses by the docks, that creepy boarded-up house in La Jolla everyone said was haunted even numerous cemeteries late at night. But we wanted something bigger, something off the grid. That's when one of my good friends, who was always scrolling through obscure forums, found a post about a ghost town deep in the desert, about a three-hour drive from home.

The post mentioned a tiny cemetery nearby, supposedly marked with weird symbols. It sounded like the perfect adventure for a weekend. A place that was weird enough and desolate enough to give us a scare but also allow us to visit a small ghost town nearby. So we drove down and decided to hike out there and check it out.

Looking back, I wish we'd never gone. There were four of us: me, Chris, Jenny, and Kevin. We were all pretty outdoorsy, used to hiking trails around Riverside or Mt Baldy, but none of us had ever done a desert trek like this. The plan was to drive out to the desert's entry point, park near a trailhead, and hike about a few miles into the desert to find the ghost town. The forum post was vague about the exact location, but a friend had pieced together some coordinates from old topographic maps and Google Earth screenshots.

We figured we'd find it eventually. The cemetery was supposed to be just beyond the town, tucked into some low foothills. The post warned about the heat and lack of water, so we packed carefully: each of us carried a 3-liter hydration bladder, plus extra gallon jugs, protein bars, dried fruit, first-aid kits, headlamps, and a couple of cheap walkie-talkies since cell service would be nonexistent.

Jenny brought her DSLR camera, and Chris had a GoPro he swore he'd use to make a YouTube video. We also tossed in some personal stuff. I had a small cross necklace I always wore, and Kevin also brought a little stone his mom gave me from a trip to Sedona, said it was "protective." We laughed about it, but he packed it anyway. We left at dawn on a Saturday in late June, the air already warm as we piled into my car. The drive out was uneventful, just us blasting music and joking about rattlesnakes and UFOs.

By 9 a.m., we'd parked at the trailhead, a dusty pull-off near a faded sign warning about dehydration risks. The desert stretched out in every direction, all jagged hills and dry washes under a sky so blue it hurt to look at. It was already pushing 90 degrees, and the heat felt like it was pressing down on us. We slathered on sunscreen, checked our maps, and started hiking. The first couple of miles were easy, following a faint trail through flat scrubland dotted with creosote bushes and the occasional barrel cactus.

But soon the path petered out, and we were navigating by compass and Kevin's handwritten notes. The foothills were trickier than they looked as loose gravel, steep inclines, and narrow ravines forced us to backtrack more than once. By noon, we were sweating through our shirts, and the water was going faster than we'd planned. We stopped in the shade of a rocky outcrop to eat and check our bearings. Chris was sure we were close, pointing out a low ridge that matched his map.

Jenny complained about blisters, and Chris kept filming everything, narrating like he was on some reality show. I remember giving him a lot of heat because it was just funny to me how he was just so serious. I tried to stay upbeat, but the desert was starting to feel endless, like it was swallowing us. Around 3 p.m., we crested a hill and saw it. Before our eyes was the ghost town.

It was smaller than I'd imagined, just a handful of crumbling buildings scattered across a dry valley. A few wooden shacks leaned crookedly, their paint long gone, windows empty like eye sockets. There was a rusted water tank tipped over, half-buried in sand, and what looked like the remains of a general store, its sign too faded to read. The place felt frozen in time, abandoned for decades, maybe longer. We dropped our packs and started exploring, our footsteps loud in the eerie quiet. Inside one building, we found broken furniture and old newspapers from the 1940s, the pages brittle and yellowed. Another had a rusted bedframe and a single shoe, which freaked Jenny out for some reason. Chris climbed onto a sagging roof to get a better shot, ignoring our yells to be careful.

There was no graffiti, no beer cans, and none of the usual signs of modern trespassers. It was like the place had been forgotten by everyone but us. As if time stood still there. Kevin was the one who found the path to the cemetery. It was barely a trail, just a faint line of packed dirt leading around a rocky hill. We grabbed our gear and followed it, the sun now dipping low, casting long shadows. The cemetery appeared suddenly, tucked into a cluster of low boulders.

It was tiny, maybe 15 or 20 graves, marked by crude wooden crosses and a few flat stones. Some had names Elias Reed, Maria Soto, dates from the 1860s and 70s. But others were blank or carved with symbols I didn't recognize. They weren't like anything I'd seen in a church or museum, more like spirals and jagged lines, almost scratched into the wood. Sarah said they looked "witchy," but Jake thought they might be old mining symbols. We took a few photos, though the light was fading, and I noticed my phone's battery was already at 20% despite being fully charged that morning.

Chris's GoPro kept glitching, too, shutting off randomly. We chalked it up to the heat. We decided to camp near one of the sturdier buildings, a small shack with three walls and half a roof. It wasn't much, but it felt safer than sleeping in the open. We gathered some dry brush and built a small campfire, careful to keep it contained in a ring of stones. Dinner was protein bars and trail mix, washed down with warm water. As the sun set, the desert turned cold fast, and we pulled on hoodies and huddled around the fire. We talked about the cemetery, trying to make sense of the symbols.

Because we knew we wouldn't have service Kevin had googled some stuff on his phone before we left, saying the town might've been a mining camp that went bust after a cave-in, but there was nothing about the cemetery. Jenny kept saying she felt weird, like we were being watched, but Kevin just teased her about being scared. I didn't say it out loud, but I felt it too. It felt like a prickling on the back of my neck, like the desert wasn't as empty as it looked. Around midnight, we started hearing noises. At first, it was just a faint rustling, like wind moving through the bushes, but there was no breeze. Then came a low hum, almost like a distant engine, but it seemed to come from the ground itself. We froze, straining to listen.

Chris grabbed his headlamp and scanned the darkness, but the beam only lit up rocks and cacti, making the shadows beyond even blacker. My flashlight was powerful, but it felt useless like the light was being swallowed by the night. The moonlight was bright enough to cast a pale glow, but it only made everything look surreal, as if we were on another planet. That's when Jenny froze and whispered, "Look over there."

We all looked as Jenny gave us a sign to be quiet. It was near the cemetery, maybe 300 yards away, that we saw them. They looked like small, bluish orbs, floating a few feet off the ground. They weren't bright, more like a faint glow, bobbing gently like they were caught in a current. There were three or four, moving in slow circles. My heart was pounding so hard I could hear it in my ears. Kevin fumbled with his phone, trying to record, but the screen froze. Jenny's camera wouldn't even turn on. My phone was dead, too, despite having battery left earlier. Chris's GoPro was useless, just a blinking red light. We turned off our headlamps, hoping the darkness would hide us, but the orbs kept drifting, never coming closer but never fading either.

We didn't dare speak, just crouched there, watching, too scared to move. Finally, we crept back to our campsite, grabbing whatever we thought might help. I clutched my cross necklace, Jenny held a rosary she'd brought, and Kevin squeezed that Sedona stone so hard it left marks on his palm.

Chris didn't have anything, but he kept muttering prayers under his breath. We packed up most of our gear, ready to bolt if we had to, but the idea of hiking a few miles in the dark was worse than staying put. The noises kept up all night—rustling, humming, and once, a sound like footsteps crunching on gravel, though nothing was there when we looked. We didn't sleep, just sat close to the dying fire, jumping at every sound. The orbs were gone by dawn, but the air still felt heavy, like something was lingering just out of sight.

We broke camp at first light, exhausted and shaken. The hike back was brutal, the heat even worse than the day before, but we didn't stop until we reached my car. None of us talked much on the way back. We just kept checking over our shoulders. When we got home, we tried to make sense of it.

Our photos from the cemetery were gone. Jenny's camera memory card was blank, and my phone had reset itself. Chris's GoPro footage was just static. Kevin found a few more forum posts about the area, mentioning "lights" and "bad energy," but nothing concrete.

We never went back, and we don't talk about it much anymore. I still have dreams of that place. What exactly was it? Was it a haunted place? Were those UFOs or Spirits? I like to think that whatever it was it belonged to that place. Forgotten in time and sifting through the desert. Sometimes I wake up thinking I hear that hum, like the desert followed me home. What were those orbs? Were the symbols in the cemetery some kind of warning? And why did our tech fail when we needed it most?

I don't have answers, but I know one thing. That place isn't as abandoned as it seems.

A Blue Flame in Brushes

I grew up in a small town surrounded by even smaller towns. It really has been a trip to see how much has changed. Where once massive farmland went on for miles, there are shopping centers and houses galore. Where once there was farmland, now lie massive home communities. It's simply crazy to me how much can change in such a short amount of time.

I remember being a young child standing in my grandparents' truck as we drove down the main road in those days. To my left and right, farmland and cows. I drive down that same street today, and I see massive home communities, shopping centers, a High School, and tons of fast food places and restaurants. Goodness, how time flies.

Despite all this, having grown up in the small towns, I grew up with a lot of the folklore surrounding these areas. My grandmother would tell me stories of how a lot of strange things would happen in the outskirts of town. My Aunt on my father's side would also tell me those same stories. So I always felt that there was a grain of truth to them. And we all know what they say about myths and folklore. Despite how crazy they may be or how off the wall they may sound. There is always a small grain of truth to them all.

When I was 18, there were still many smaller towns surrounding the town where I grew up. They weren't nearly as developed as they are now. The town in this ghastly experience was a speck on the map at the time. A place where stories lingered in the wind and the past felt as close as the shadow at your back. As I mentioned, I was young and often went where the world was a mystery to be unraveled. My friends and I at that time were hungry for adventure and often went wherever the winds took us. Perhaps it was the local folklore or maybe just something to break the monotony of small-town life. Funny as I say, small town life. Because it isnt a small town anymore. But I digress.

Growing up, when I would visit my second cousin's ranch, she would tell us stories of this hidden grove of trees not far from her home. Now her mother owned a very large section of property, which consisted of multiple acres of land in the area. It varied from many apricot trees to small bushes and trees. There were many acres, most of which were set up for farming, but still a vast amount of it wasn't fully cleaned out for much of anything but wild trees and bushes.

In one small section, far off in the distance, there was a place. We all walked to it once. The air was just different there. It seemed like an odd collection of trees surrounded by bushes. My Cousin called it The Grove. In the center, we could see burnt wax and what looked like feathers. We didn't think much of it and simply seemed to forget about it as time flew by. A few months later, while my mother was visiting, my second cousin and I were talking about some of these rumors.

She spun tales of how late at night, under certain phases of the moon, she would see shimmering blue and green lights coming from the grove on her daily walks with her dogs around her property. While her property was still a good way away from the grove, she still had that line of sight to it. She never got close enough to it, though. As she didn't want her dogs to make any noise or disrupt what may have been going on.

Back then, there was a lot of satanic stuff running around in local newspapers and the news. In my eyes, pretty much everything I owned was satanic growing up. This was due largely to the influence of my Grandparents who were very religious. My

He-Mans, Transformers, etc., were all considered evil in nature. Oh, how I still cry knowing how much those toys are worth now. But I digress. I was older now, and these stories intrigued me.

As the years progressed and time flew by, my fascination with these things intensified. It wasn't until I was around eighteen years of age that my friends and I started actively pursuing these things. One night, while playing with the Ouija board, rumors of that old grove resurfaced. It was the one near my cousin's home. Talk of a foreboding place where rituals were performed under the cloak of darkness had reached our ears. Skeptical but intrigued, we decided to investigate the grove, a hidden enclave of trees that held secrets in their roots and whispers in their leaves.

In the broad daylight, we found it: an opening in the woods, a clearing that felt like stepping into another world. Strange markings scored the earth, and stones were arranged in patterns that made my skin prickle with unease. The place felt off, as if we were intruders in a space that was not meant for us. Yet, the sun was a comforting presence, a reminder that we were still tethered to reality.

We left as the shadows grew long, but the grove called to us, an unanswered question that gnawed at our curiosity. We had to return, we decided, under the shroud of night. And so we did. The grove was transformed in the darkness, the trees now sentinels watching our every move. A blue light flickered in the distance, an unnatural hue that seemed to pulse with a life of its own. We parked my car and moved towards the grove with the stealth of hunters, our hearts pounding a frantic rhythm.

Hiding behind trees and rocks, we peered through binoculars and saw them: figures robed in cloaks, their faces obscured, gathered in a circle. They chanted in a language that twisted the air, and at the center of their circle, a flame burned blue, a beacon in the night.

A sense of evil washed over us, a palpable force that whispered of danger. We retreated, our steps careful to avoid the crack of a twig or the rustle of leaves that might betray our presence. We made it back to the safety of our cars, the grove now a memory that clung to us like a cold fog. We drove away, but the experience remained, a story we would recount in hushed tones.

Years have passed, and the grove is no more, replaced by homes and the laughter of children. But sometimes, when the night is still, we wonder if the residents ever feel a chill, a momentary unease, as if the land remembers the rituals that once claimed it as their own.

The Lake of Secrets

It was supposed to be an adventure, a break from the monotony of everyday life. Samantha and I had packed our gear with excitement, eager for the weekend camping trip near the Mexico border. The lake, Lago Escondido, was a hidden gem about two hours away, its waters gleaming like a sapphire amidst the arid landscape.

Me and Sam were great friends. We'd often head down to Joshua Tree, camp all night near a small fire, and gawk at the fantastic night sky. We'd often see that the stars were most bright when the arm of the Milky Way Galaxy was at its zenith. A site for all to witness for sure. But what made our friendship special was our love for randomly getting out and finding good places to eat or camping to get away from that SoCal life.

We were anxious to get started when we discovered and heard about Lake Escondido. We packed the necessities and drove down. We arrived just before dusk, the sky painted in hues of fiery orange and purple. The lake was calm, and the air was filled with the scent of pine and earth. We set up our tent in a small clearing, surrounded by whispering trees, unaware of the stories that clung to the place like the moss on the rocks.

While the entire campsite was captivating, it wasn't an isolated area. There were tons of other sites with many families and adults scattered around. The lake had a small trail, but it was clearly visible from all the campsites in our area.

My friend and I spent a few hours setting up our site, unloading our car, and getting ready for our first night there. We had so much fun that night. We smoked some cigars, cooked up some smores on the fire, and just sat there telling stories and breathing in the fresh air.

When nightfall came, we were surprised that the weather wasn't that cold. So we grabbed a nice blanket and some padding and laid down, gazing at the stars above. My friend told me some cool stories she had heard as a kid, and I also shared mine. As we gazed above at the clear night sky, we saw tons of shooting stars. The night was truly magical—a far cry from what was to come a few nights later.

The next day, we went hiking, following a trail that hugged the lake's edge. That's when we found them—strange markings etched into the boulders, symbols that seemed ancient and out of place. They were like whispers from the past, and I felt a chill despite the warm sun on my back. We both looked at the markings in awe. How old were they? We pondered how long they may have been there and even laughed, thinking that perhaps it was just some modern graffiti that someone could have done to make it seem old.

Regardless, these markings kind of gave us the spooks. They just didn't seem natural-looking—more occultist than anything. Regardless, we carried on and saw a lone hiker walking towards us. He was a normal-looking fellow, probably in his 60s, but he seemed nice. He told us the lake was beautiful and even suggested a good area to swim in, as the lake was off limits to swimming, as there weren't any lifeguards around.

We continued onward and eventually found the place the older man told us about. We began to take off our clothes, revealing our swimsuits, and we swam to a little island at the center of the lake. It was there that we discovered old arrowheads and more intricate and deliberate carvings. The artifacts spoke of a time long forgotten, and I couldn't shake the feeling that we were not alone.

We swam around a bit more and then made our way back. We dried off our towels and laid on a nice slab of rock, just taking in the gentle breeze, fresh air, and warmth of the sun in the clear skies. It wasn't long before we headed back. We were having a great time, but at night, the true nature of Lago Escondido revealed itself.

As the evening began, we again made a nice fire. We could hear the people laughing and singing away, as most families do. We laughed and joked. After a few drinks and eating some smoked sausages, we went to our tent. Again, we cuddled and told each other stories. We eventually passed out. That's when it happened. It was very quiet at first. There was no singing from families as it was late now. As we lay in our tent, the silence was shattered by inexplicable noises—rustling, whispers, and a faint drumming that seemed to come from the depths of the earth. I'd say it was around 3 a.m. when we heard those first noises.

We then saw shadows dancing on the sides of our eyes on the canvas of our tent, forming shapes that defied logic. It was odd, though, because when we would turn, nothing would be there. Things would seem normal, but when we tried to fall back asleep, we would hear noises again, and the shadows at the corners of our eyes resumed.

Thinking someone was lurking around our tent. I grabbed a flashlight, and we both walked out, and nothing. Every other site was pitch black. Everyone seemed as if they were asleep. We did some some small light coming from some tents but no movement. We thought it was nothing, so we went back into our tent.

We zipped it up, decided our minds were playing tricks, and tried to fall asleep. About 30 minutes into lying there and talking to each other, we heard scampering around our tent. No, it wasn't the kind you hear from animals. These sounded like children running around.

We again summoned up some courage and walked out with flashlights in hand. That's when we noticed the footprints. No one was near us, yet the ground around our tent was marred with bizarre, inhuman footprints. They encircled our shelter, and to our horror, we found prints scaling the fabric of our tent.

Last night, the air was thick and tense. We heard the soft tread of footsteps and the murmur of voices speaking a language we couldn't understand. The footprints returned, but this time, they led into the water, disappearing beneath the moonlit ripples.

We left at dawn, the lake now a mirror of secrets. We never spoke of what happened, but sometimes, I can hear the faint drumming when the night is still. I wonder about the mysteries of Lago Escondido and the spirits that linger there.

It wasn't until a year later, on a chilly autumn evening at her home, that we finally discussed the trip to the lake. As we sat by the crackling fire, we began our research. We discovered that the lake was notorious for being one of the most haunted locations in California, with chilling tales of strange sounds and mysterious sightings.

It's hard to believe we unknowingly stepped into such a terrifying and haunted place. Did we stumble upon something dark and sinister lurking just beneath the surface? We might never know for sure, as we made a pact never to return—a vow forged in fear. Some experiences are better left untouched, locked away in the shadows. Yet, even now, I can't shake the haunting "what if?"

Angels in the Light: Divine Affirmations After the Shadows

After recounting those early wanderings into forbidden practices and places, the brushes with darkness that left me spiritually broken, and the merciful intervention of death and resurrection through Covid where God pulled me back from the brink, I thought my story of transformation was complete. I had surrendered fully to Jesus Christ, allowing Him to steer my life, and I focused on living in His light rather than dwelling on the shadows.

But God, in His infinite grace, doesn't stop at rescue. He continues to reveal Himself, to strengthen what He has begun, even years later. In the time since my healing and renewed walk, two extraordinary encounters with angels. Both undeniable, awe-filled moments straight from heaven that have pushed my faith deeper into the heart of Jesus Christ than I ever imagined possible. These weren't relics of the past; they were fresh confirmations that the God who saved me is still actively at work, sending His messengers to guide, protect, and affirm.

These visitations brought peace, clarity, and an overwhelming sense of His presence, reminding me that faith isn't a one-time event but a living journey. They also stirred reflections on the deeper roots of my story where this unshakeable trust truly originated. That foundation lies in my mother's own powerful walk with the Lord, a testimony so profound it shaped everything that followed in our family. Her experiences, battles, and triumphs hold the keys to understanding how faith became our anchor.

Moreover, as I navigated the brokenness of our healthcare system, endless denials, delays, pain, and uncertainty it was this same faith in Jesus, fueled by prayer and divine strength, that carried me through. What the world called impossible, God made possible.

What follows are those angelic encounters. Not as ancient miracles, but as recent proofs that the Light still breaks through, pursuing us relentlessly. They lead us straight to the heart: my mother's full story, the source from which so much grace has flowed.

The Stranger in the Elevator

In the years since God raised me from death during Covid, I'd learned to trust His hand more deeply. Yet life doesn't stop testing that trust. Last year, my mom faced her own battle. A battle that is currently on going. During a routine Emergency Room Visit for a Urinary Tract Infection things happened that shook my newborn faith to its core. What happened blew my mind and gave me an even greater purpose. To be a strong advocate for my mother amongst a broken healthcare system. But I knew it would be tough and I knew I needed something to help me. During her ER visit it turned into her getting admitted to the ICU, freshly tracheotomized after complications that no one saw coming. The weight of it all pressed hard. I'd fought the broken healthcare system tooth and nail for my own survival, witnessing God's wisdom and provision punch through impossible barriers. Now, watching her suffer, I felt that old helplessness creep back in. I knew what God had done for me, but in the chaos of machines beeping, doctors' guarded words, and endless waiting, I somehow forgot: He is still in control. He always has been.

One late evening, exhausted and heavy-hearted, I walked toward the hospital's front doors. The entrance was eerily empty. No visitors, no staff bustling, nope just me and the quiet hum of fluorescent lights. As I approached, a man walked up at the same moment. We were the only two souls there. We stepped into the elevator together.

Something felt... off. Not threatening, but different. He kept glancing at me, studying me with calm intensity. In the confined space, the air thickened. Then he spoke.

"I know you."

I blinked. "You do?"

He nodded slowly. "Yes, I do. You have a very powerful and wonderful testimony, don't you?"

My heart skipped. How? My book *Learning to Fly* shares my Covid journey, and my photo is in it, but

I'd never done big public speaking only shared with friends, family, and small groups the Lord led me to. Caring for Mom had consumed everything else. No crowds, no fame. Yet here was this stranger, naming it exactly.

As the elevator rose, he smiled gently. I managed a smile back. When the doors opened on my floor, I extended my hand. "God is good."

He took it firmly, then stepped closer, locking eyes with mine. In that instant, his eyes shifted colors, changing in a way that's hard to describe, like a veil lifted, revealing something eternal, profound. He held my gaze and said, "God is good. Don't you *ever* forget that."

I stepped off, stunned. The doors closed behind me. I stood frozen in the hallway, replaying it. How did he know? Strangers don't say those things. And those eyes... they weren't ordinary.

Then, like a warm wave, peace flooded in. Inside my spirit, clear as a whisper: *I am always with you.*

In that moment, I knew from the bottom of my heart that God was with my mom. He had been all along. The battles with the system, the fear, the helplessness they didn't just stop with me nor did they change the truth: He is in control. He sends reminders when we need them most, sometimes through the most unexpected of messengers.

This encounter wasn't the end of the trial, but it was a turning point. It reminded me that faith isn't just for survival it's for every step, every worry, every hospital hallway. And it pointed me back to the source of that enduring strength: my mother's own walk with the Lord, a story far bigger than mine, one that would soon unfold and reveal how God's faithfulness runs through generations.

The Priest and the Relic

Nearly a year after the trach placement and the elevator encounter that reminded me God is always with us, my mom was now in a sub-acute facility in San Leandro, adjusting to 24/7 trach care. Life had stabilized somewhat, but the battles with her health—and our broken healthcare system—continued. Then, on the morning of January 3, 2026, breathing difficulties hit hard. She was rushed by ambulance to the hospital.

A critical EMT error sent her to the county facility instead of her primary hospital—a mistake that infuriated me at first. But as always, God was in control. That very night, she was transferred to her primary hospital in Redwood City, exactly where she needed to be.

A few days later, a priest walked into her room. Unbeknownst to him, a few weeks earlier my aunt had given me a rosary blessed by the Pope at the Vatican in Rome. My mom, deeply Catholic, had always loved praying the rosary. For months, I'd been praying the Divine Mercy Chaplet over her daily—a powerful prayer my grandma (her mom) used in dire times. My aunt reminded me of its origins: Jesus Himself commissioned it to a Polish nun, Sister Faustina Kowalska, in the 1930s. He dictated the words, promising extraordinary graces—mercy for souls, healing, protection. Through the Chaplet, you plead: "For the sake of His sorrowful Passion, have mercy on us and on the whole world." It's known for its immense power, especially at the hour of mercy (3:00 p.m.), and I'd clung to it relentlessly for Mom.

I shared this with the priest. He listened, impressed. "There really isn't any prayer stronger I could offer over her," he said.

Then he paused, opened his bag, and pulled out a beautiful Miraculous Medal attached to a bracelet. "This has touched the tomb of Sister Faustina in Poland," he explained. He'd been there just weeks ago—something stirred him to buy it at the Shrine of Divine Mercy in Kraków-Łagiewniki, where her remains rest in the chapel beneath the miraculous image of Merciful Jesus.

"I think this is meant for you," he said.

I was shaken. "I can't accept that."

"No," he insisted gently. "It's for you. It always was."

Together, we prayed over Mom—the Divine Mercy Chaplet, the rosary, invoking Jesus' mercy. He left, and I never saw him again during her stay.

Think about it: I'd been praying this exact prayer non-stop. The rosary from the Vatican tied into Divine Mercy. The priest, fresh from Poland, brings a relic touched to Faustina's own tomb—precisely when Mom needed heavenly reinforcement. And none of it happens without that "mistake" routing her to the right place.

There are no coincidences. No accidents. God orchestrates every detail—down to a priest's impulse purchase halfway around the world—to show His power, glory, and mercy through our Lord Jesus Christ.

That bracelet now stays close to me, a tangible reminder of heaven's mercy touching earth. The Divine Mercy Chaplet, born from Christ's own words to St. Faustina, carried us through the storm and continues to do so. It has reinforced my faith in ways I can't fully express—showing me the power, glory, and endless mercy of our Lord Jesus Christ.

But my mother's complete story—the depths of her own walk with the Lord, the prayers she prayed, the grace she carried through her trials—is far too vast and profound for these pages. That testimony deserves its own book, one that will unfold in time. For now, let's turn to the prayer that became my anchor during those hardest days: the Chaplet of Divine Mercy. What follows is a dedicated chapter on how to pray it, the full prayers involved, and why it holds such power for anyone seeking God's mercy.

The Chaplet of Divine Mercy

The Divine Mercy Chaplet isn't just a prayer—it's a lifeline Jesus Himself gave to the world through St. Faustina Kowalska, a Polish nun in the 1930s. He appeared to her, commissioning her to record His messages and spread devotion to His Divine Mercy. The Chaplet pleads for mercy "for the sake of His sorrowful Passion," and Jesus promised extraordinary graces to those who pray it with trust.

In my darkest moments—caring for Mom in the hospital, fighting the broken system, feeling helpless—I clung to this prayer daily. My grandma had prayed it in times of need, my aunt reminded me of its power and gave me the Vatican-blessed rosary to use with it, and then the priest brought the relic from Faustina's tomb. No coincidences. This prayer became my daily weapon, filling me with peace and deeper faith in Jesus.

Jesus made beautiful promises to those who pray it faithfully (from St. Faustina's Diary): Whoever recites it will receive great mercy at the hour of death.

Priests will recommend it to sinners as their last hope.

Even the most hardened sinner, if they recite it once, will receive grace from His infinite mercy.

When said for the dying, He stands between them and the Father as the Merciful Savior, not the just Judge.

Souls who spread this devotion won't experience terror at death; His mercy will shield them.

These aren't empty words—they're Christ's direct assurances. Pray it especially at 3:00 p.m. (the Hour of Mercy, recalling His death on the Cross).

How to Pray the Chaplet of Divine Mercy Use a standard rosary (five decades). It takes about 10-15 minutes.

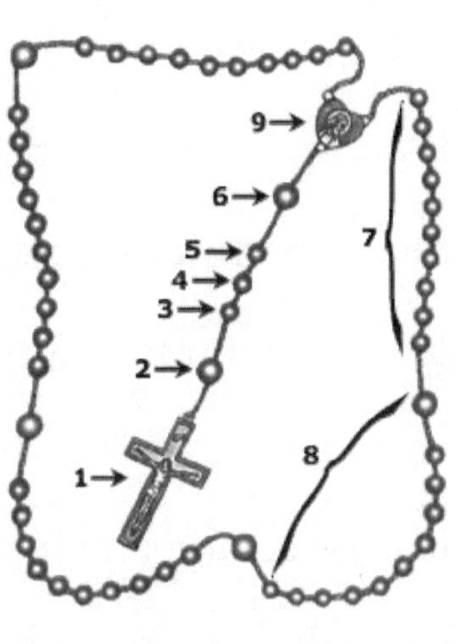

1. Make the Sign of the Cross

In the name of the Father, and of the Son, and of the Holy Spirit. Amen.

2. Optional Opening Prayers

St. Faustina's Prayer for Sinners

O Jesus, eternal Truth, our Life, I call upon You and I beg Your mercy for poor sinners. O sweetest Heart of my Lord, full of pity and unfathomable mercy, I plead with You for poor sinners. O Most Sacred Heart, Fount of Mercy from which gush forth rays of inconceivable graces upon the entire human race, I beg of You light for poor sinners. O Jesus, be mindful of Your own bitter Passion and do not permit the loss of souls redeemed at so dear a price of Your most precious Blood. O Jesus, when I consider the great price of Your Blood, I rejoice at its immensity, for one drop alone would have been enough for the salvation of all sinners. Although sin is an abyss of wickedness and ingratitude, the price paid for us can never be equalled. Therefore, let every soul trust in the Passion of the Lord, and place its hope in His mercy. God will not deny His mercy to anyone. Heaven and earth may change, but God's mercy will never be exhausted. Oh, what immense joy burns in my heart when I contemplate Your incomprehensible goodness, O Jesus! I desire to bring all sinners to Your feet that they may glorify Your mercy throughout endless ages.

You expired, Jesus, but the source of life gushed forth for souls, and the ocean of mercy opened up for the whole world. O Fount of Life, unfathomable Divine Mercy, envelop the whole world and empty Yourself out upon us.

(Repeat three times)

O Blood and Water, which gushed forth from the Heart of Jesus as a fount of mercy for us, I trust in You!

3. Our Father

Our Father, Who art in Heaven, hallowed be Thy name; Thy kingdom come; Thy will be done on earth as it is in Heaven. Give us this day our daily bread; and forgive us our trespasses, as we forgive those who trespass against us; and lead us not into temptation, but deliver us from evil, Amen.

4. Hail Mary

Hail Mary, full of grace. The Lord is with thee. Blessed art thou amongst women, and blessed is the fruit of thy womb, Jesus. Holy Mary, Mother of God, pray for us sinners, now and at the hour of our death, Amen.

5. The Apostles' Creed

I believe in God, the Father almighty, Creator of Heaven and earth, and in Jesus Christ, His only Son, our Lord, who was conceived by the Holy Spirit, born of the Virgin Mary, suffered under Pontius Pilate, was crucified, died and was buried; He descended into hell; on the third day He rose again from the dead; He ascended into Heaven, and is seated at the right hand of God the Father almighty; from there He will come to judge the living and the dead. I believe in the Holy Spirit, the holy Catholic Church, the Communion of Saints, the forgiveness of sins, the Resurrection of the body, and life everlasting. Amen.

6. The Eternal Father

Eternal Father, I offer You the Body and Blood, Soul and Divinity of Your Dearly Beloved Son, Our Lord, Jesus Christ, in atonement for our sins and those of the whole world.

7. On the 10 Small Beads of Each Decade

For the sake of His sorrowful Passion, have mercy on us and on the whole world.

8. Repeat for the remaining decades

Saying the "Eternal Father" (6) on the "Our Father" bead and then 10 "For the sake of His sorrowful Passion" (7) on the following "Hail Mary" beads.

9. Conclude with Holy God (Repeat three times)

Holy God, Holy Mighty One, Holy Immortal One, have mercy on us and on the whole world.

10. Optional Closing Prayers

Eternal God, in Whom mercy is endless and the treasury of compassion — inexhaustible, look kindly upon us and increase Your mercy in us, that in difficult moments we might not despair nor become despondent, but with great confidence submit ourselves to Your holy will, which is Love and Mercy itself.

O Greatly Merciful God, Infinite Goodness, today all mankind calls out from the abyss of its misery to Your mercy — to Your compassion, O God; and it is with its mighty voice of misery that it cries out. Gracious God, do not reject the prayer of this earth's exiles! O Lord, Goodness beyond our understanding, Who are acquainted with our misery through and through, and know that by our own power we cannot ascend to You, we implore You: anticipate us with Your grace and keep on increasing Your mercy in us, that we may faithfully do Your holy will all through our life and at death's hour. Let the omnipotence of Your mercy shield us from the darts of our salvation's enemies, that we may with confidence, as Your children, await Your [Son's] final coming — that day known to You alone. And we expect to obtain everything promised us by Jesus in spite of all our wretchedness. For Jesus is our Hope: through His merciful Heart, as through an open gate, we pass through to Heaven.

Pray it with your heart open to Jesus' mercy. It changed everything for me—turning fear into trust, helplessness into hope. If you're facing trials, try it. Let it draw you closer to Christ, just as it did for me and my family.

This prayer prepared my heart for whatever came next, including the full story of my mom's powerful journey and testimony which I'll share in its own book someday soon.

Afterword

After reading about my past, I invite you to join me in the next chapter of my journey - Learning to Fly: Surviving Covid-19.

I faced the most challenging battle of my life when I contracted the worst case of Covid-19 the hospital had ever seen. Despite needing CPR to revive my heart, I overcame the odds and made an incredible recovery. But I had help. My lord and Savior, Jesus Christ, was right there with me every step of the way.

Which is why I was enticed to write this book. I wanted to show the dangers of falling out of faith while dabbling with occult-type things. While you are free to choose or debate what I've written, I know my experience wasn't fake, and it serves as a warning to those in a similar position.

There are things we simply can not explain. We should leave things alone while focusing on the one true thing that matters. We should love and honor Jesus and live the life he wishes for us to live. I've learned that now and am happy and excited about what the future holds for me.

Though these experiences are my own it was my faith in Jesus Christ that ultimately delivered me. I've seen so many miracles and I encourge you all to seek Jesus when you need him. I also strongly encourage you build your relationship. See it shouldn't be that we only seek him when we need him but that we also thank him when things are going well.

God is always with us and if anything, the story of how i rekindled my faith and the power prayer my only hope is that you the reader are inspired to do the same. I hope to encourage others to focus on their will to thrive, have faith in God, believe without doubt, and maintain a relentless attitude to achieve the impossible.

About the Author

Michael Andrews was born and raised in the East Bay Area of California. Growing up, he loved writing stories and making his own Choose Your Own Adventure Stories, often writing and sharing them with friends who loved them.

An avid writer of Horror, Fantasy, Sci-Fi, and Adventure, He is the Author of the award-winning and best-selling book "Tales from the Starlight Kingdom" and creator of The Curator Evolving Universe.

He would later pursue his writing career in Southern California. While writing, Michael also enjoyed a career as a Game Developer and tester, often appearing at numerous conventions and events.

Fate would eventually lead him back to Northern California to tend to the care of his mother. Upon his return, Michael battled against one of the worst cases of COVID-19 in the entire San Francisco Bay Area.

Making one of the most miraculous recoveries in the hospital's history and writing an award-winning autobiography "Learning to Fly – Surviving Covid-19, he now travels across California, giving his testimony of the power of true faith in God and what true determination and willpower can do.

Michael is also an activist within the East Bay, fighting for a better healthcare system and has also appeared on "The War Room" with Rich Bannon and on a few influencer's YouTube Channels.

You can learn more about Michael Andrews by visiting his website and social media links below.

www.themichaelandrews.com

www.soseverestudios.com

Twitter: @So_Severe

Facebook.com/0Michael.Andrews

Michael Andrews

THE SOSEVERE EXPERIENCE

Appendix : Prayers of Protection

Listed below are a few prayers to help protect you in your time of need. Some of these are staples that I continue using to this very day. I hope that if anything, these prayers bring you comfort and spiritual protection.

Under the Protection of the Most High

Father, I want to live in the shadow of Your wing. When life is hard, and I don't know what to do, help me remember that You are with me and that I am never alone. I cannot live without You. I cannot face tomorrow without the promise of Your presence. Today I choose to walk and live under the protection of You, The Most High. In Jesus' Name, Amen.

Prayer for the Protection of Family

†

Lord, I pray Your emotional, physical, and spiritual protection over my kids (grandkids). Keep evil far from them, and help them to trust You as their refuge and strength. I pray You will guard their minds from harmful instruction and grant them discernment to recognize truth.

I pray You will make them strong and courageous in the presence of danger, recognizing that You have overcome and will set right all injustice and wrong one day. Help them find rest in Your shadow as they live in the spiritual shelter You provide them. Let them know that the only safe place is in Jesus and that their home on earth is only temporary. Amen.

A Prayer to Guard Against Spiritual Attacks

We know that the enemy wouldn't be fighting so hard against us if we weren't making a difference for your Kingdom. He wouldn't be trying so hard to stop us if he didn't think you had so much good still in store. Remind us today, Lord, that the battle belongs to you, and whatever we're up against can be taken down in one fell swoop by your mighty hand. Please help us to trust you more, to stop wasting time just spinning our wheels or fighting in our strength.

Forgive us for the times we've neglected to set our eyes and hearts on you, for the days we've forgotten to come to you first. Fill us with the power of your Holy Spirit. Fill us with your wisdom and discernment to make us aware of the enemy's traps, so we can stand strong against his schemes. Thank you for your constant reminders that your presence will go with us in whatever we face, and you will give us rest. Amen.

Protection from Temptation

O Christ, Son of God, for our sake, you fasted forty days and allowed yourself to be tempted. Protect us so that we may not be led astray by any temptation. Since man does not live by bread alone, nourish our souls with the heavenly food of your Word; through your mercy, O our God, you are blessed and live and govern all things, now and forever. Amen.

Armor of God Prayer

Dear God, today we put on the full armor to guard our lives against attack. We put on the belt of truth to protect against lies and deception. We put on the breastplate of righteousness to protect our hearts from the temptations we battle. We put the gospel of peace on our feet, so we're ready to take your light wherever you send us this day. We choose to walk in the peace and freedom of your Spirit and not be overcome with fear and anxious thoughts. We take up your shield of faith that will extinguish all the darts and threats hurled our way by the enemy.

We believe in your power to protect us and choose to trust in you. We put on the helmet of salvation, which covers our minds and thoughts, reminding us we are children of the day, forgiven, set free, and saved by the grace of Christ Jesus. We take up the sword of the Spirit, your very Word, the one offensive weapon given to us for battle, which has the power to demolish strongholds, alive, active, and sharper than any double-edged sword.

We ask for your help in remembering to put on your full armor every day, for you give us all that we need to stand firm in this world. Forgive us,

God, for the times we've been unprepared, too busy to care, or trying to fight and wrestle in our own strength.

Thank you that we never fight alone, for you are constantly at work on our behalf, shielding, protecting, strengthening, exposing deeds of darkness, bringing to light what needs to be known, covering us from the cruel attacks we face even when we're unaware, in the powerful name of Jesus, Amen.

The Our Father Prayer

Our Father who art in heaven, hallowed be thy name. Thy kingdom come. Thy will be done on earth as it is in heaven. Give us this day our daily bread, and forgive us our trespasses, as we forgive those who trespass against us, and lead us not into temptation, but deliver us from evil. For thine is the kingdom and the power, and the glory, forever and ever. Amen

www.ingramcontent.com/pod-product-compliance
Lightning Source LLC
LaVergne TN
LVHW091144080826
845145LV00008B/2248

* 9 7 8 1 7 3 7 6 7 2 9 3 7 *